*Dan and Jane,*
*A story for all years.*
*Dan D.*

# *Passages From Our Times*

An essay-drama of American history

1998–2010

# Dan Donovan

ORIGINAL WRITING

© 2008 Dan Donovan

All characters appearing in this work are fictitious. Any resemblance to real persons, living or dead, is coincidental.

All rights reserved. No part of this publication may be reproduced in any form or by any means—graphic, electronic or mechanical, including photocopying, recording, taping or information storage and retrieval systems—without the prior written permission of the author.

ISBN: 978-1-906018-47-4

A CIP catalogue for this book is available from the National Library.

Published by Original Writing Ltd., Dublin, 2008.

Printed in Ireland.

# Author's Note

THIS STORY IS WRITTEN as if it were a book being done by a character within the story. He is James Patrick Kilmurry, and in the story he is the political editor of The New York Chronicle. This newspaper is fictitious. The principal characters are loosely based on American political figures. What are described as past events reflect a "what if" history of America and the world.

James Patrick Kilmurry would describe the work this way :

The format presented in this book is essay-drama. This combines the standard presentation features of an essay with "created" scenes involving private conversations or other non-publicized events. Such scenes are not fictional because they are based upon interviews with one or more of the participants, or with individuals closely associated with one or more of the participants, or on diaries or written notes maintained by a participant and made available to this writer. In these scenes, what is presented as a quote must be understood to be a reasonable reconstruction of thoughts expressed based on a participant's recollection, or a knowledgeable assumption by an informed associate of the participant.

Other books by the James Patrick Kilmurry include:

*The Green Flag Of Liberty"—Ireland's successful 1798 war for independence.*

*"The Cornerstone For The New Millennium"—Tracing America's history from the States' War (1861-1867) through the Proxy War era (1949-1991).*

*Tell me a tale of stem or stone, beside the rivering waters of, hither and thithering waters of, night.*

—James Joyce

*Disorder always increases with time.*

—Ludwig Boltzmann

# *Prologue*

## Trans-Millennium

FEW MOMENTOUS EVENTS spring full-grown onto the stage of history. They begin almost without exception in occurrences that were left unchecked as the impact of their effects multiplied exponentially. The period referred to as the Trans-Millennium (1998–2002) bore witness to an array of happenstances which could have been effectively dealt with by the United States if its Government had not been mired in the morass of the Raft Investment Services debacle, and then the sectarian warfare that engulfed Basraistan.

The Raft scandal became the focal point of the De Witt Administration, excluding all other major issues from thoughtful, full-time consideration by any senior Administration official. The conflict in West Asia passed unresolved to the successor Administration.

America's involvement in the latest West Asia conflict resulted from its participation in ending a previous war in the region; the 1990–1991 Gulf War had seen Iran invade Iraq and Kuwait, but a US-led alliance of 50 nations ousted the invasion forces. The regimes in Iran and Iraq (both thuggish dictatorships that had fought each other previously) were not changed. However, the borders of both nations were redrawn in the hope of ending sectarian animosities.

The victorious allied leadership based their map revisions creating Kurdistan (from former northern Iraq/western Iran), Basraistan—for the Shia Moslems (from former southern Iraq) and Khuzestan- for an Arab minority that had been in neo-Persian dominated western Iran, on the 1947 plan by the then recently established League of Nations to redraw the maps of Palestine and The Levant according to data compiled in a family-by-family census of the region; this plan was endorsed by the three major religions born in West Asia. Each permitted their universal symbol (the Star, the Good Shepard, the Crescent) to be displayed on the cover of the document. Despite occasional skirmishes among radicals, the 1947 Geneva Accord has kept the peace for the five new countries in what could have been a volatile region. The 1992 plan for West Asia, tragically, was not as successful.

Raft Investment Services became a topic for discussion among the general public when the Federal Grand Jury indictments were handed down on February 30, 1998.

[In this history the months April through August have 31 days and September through March have 30 days.]

The indictments alleged that a score of individuals working in, or in conjunction with, the De Witt Administration, acting alone or in concert, by deeds of commission and/or omission, sought to sidetrack, obfuscate and/or obstruct the several investigations into the originating circumstances of, and the intended purposes of, the attempts at record revisions involving the financial affairs of the De Witt family vis-à-vis Raft Investment Services prior to Jeffrey De Witt's assumption of office as President of the United States on January 20, 1993. Raft had declared bankruptcy despite a considerable deposit of funds by the State Employees' Pension Plan in Mr. De Witt's home State. He had acted as a financial consultant to Raft, while another member of the family served as the State's Attorney General. The Federal investigation had been conducted initially in 1993 (and quite ineffectively) by the Department of Justice, then a brace of Congressional committees, and finally by the Office of the Independent Counsel.

The subject had originally come to light during the 1992 Presidential campaign in an off-handed manner. This writer had travelled to Faith, Louisiana to interview childhood acquaintances of a successful local favorite—former Mayor, then U.S. Senator and now candidate for President, Jeffrey Monroe De Witt. Sitting amid a gathering of folks in the town's coffee shop, this writer had asked several general questions. The replies kept coming around to financial planning schemes emanating from a company known as Raft Investment Services. The De Witt Family was one of the general partners. There was talk of failing Savings and Loan Associations being purchased at bargain prices, of property acquisitions signed and done before the hint of a pending sale was made public, and of unsecured loans from businesses to the local political hierarchy. This writer's columns were laughed off by De Witt as "the by-product of the joshing of a Yankee by some good ol' boys." It is well known how the issue flared, faltered, stirred again, sizzled again, and stalled again over the next two years.

When the opposition Federalist Party took control of both Houses of Congress following the 1994 elections the issue was back in the spotlight. The Federal investigation was still attempting to set up shop, and was led only by a Deputy Assistant U.S. Attorney. Congressional committees took control in January 1995 and established the Office of the Independent Counsel to complete the work.

What was eventually discovered concerning the cover-up of Mr. De Witt's involvement showed that the transgressions which transpired prior to Mr. De Witt's Inauguration Day were dwarfed by the subsequent Byzantine subterfuge created to deflect any and all outside perusals of matters relating to Raft Investment Services.

At this point to relate in detail that the naming of that most notable of non-governmental figures as the pre-eminent director in every stage of the conspiracy, and that her presence at the Defence table during the three month trial paralyzed American society in a paroxysm of macabre fascination and mournful detestation would indeed seem the reopening of old wounds. Her conviction, the subsequent first-ever Presidential resignation (brought about by the firestorm of protest following the Executive pardon), and the assumption of the Presidency by a career politician whose success in public life was owed to private connections only fed the downward spiral of the citizens' contempt for politics.

Jeffrey De Witt's resignation as President on September 8, 1998 brought his two-time running mate, former Florida Governor Gregory Albertson, into the Oval Office almost certainly against his better judgement. The De Witt—Albertson team had defeated incumbent President Milton Prescott in the 1992 election primarily on economic issues born of a harsh recession. Unbelievably, the Alliance triumph over Iran played no part in the campaign debate; Prescott tossed away his best cards in the self-delusion that the public was no longer concerned with the issue of global security.

De Witt and Albertson had run as the nominal candidates of the Libertarian Party; but, essentially, they conducted themselves as independents. This, however, did not save their party from the voters' wrath when the economy failed to improve. As a result of the 1994 Congressional elections, the Federalist Party took control of both chambers for the first time in several decades. The new Speaker of the House of Representatives, Todd Poorberry of California, made a personal commitment to unearth every last detail of the Raft scandal.

Greg Albertson had been a little-known member of the State Assembly before being elected Governor. His claim to fame was endorsing, at a critical time, a growing protest movement which sought to block a proposal by the entertainment conglomerate Willie Datbow Productions. The firm wanted to purchase ownership of the city of St. Augustine (site of the earliest permanent European settlement in the Western Hemisphere). Datbow envisioned transforming the city into a live-in, work-in theme park centered on Native American and Spanish colonialism heritage. Free enterprise zealots saw nothing wrong with a plastic-coated travesty, provided investors could make a profit. Community groups, environmentalists and historians rallied against the concept. A series of articles by The Saturday Evening Post focused widespread attention on Albertson's offer of pro bono legal representation for those opposing Datbow. The increasingly adverse opinion climate embarrassed Datbow into withdrawing its plans.

Greg Albertson's contribution to the Administration he served as Vice President was his ability to do as he was told. Despite the usual blather about making the Veep a key player for the in-coming Government, Albertson found himself simply chairing several flash-in-the-pan committees on procedural bureaucratic functions. As he took up his new responsibility as Chief Executive, Albertson became appalled at how truly critical foreign affairs had become—especially its influence on the economy; and, how truly little the heldover advisers from his predecessor knew about formulating an effective response to several developing crises.

After 1994 the De Witt Administration was essentially on cruise control. The only item which stirred its attention away from Raft damage mitigation was its 1996 re-election effort. This undertaking was greatly aided by the flawed style offered by the Federalist candidate, Iowa Governor Ben Sunkist. Despite being a highly decorated veteran of the US-NATO Expeditionary Force during the 1949–1951 Balkans War, and having served five terms as Governor, Sunkist lacked the theatrical ability possessed by Jeff De Witt to emotionally present himself as the stellar advocate of whatever topic endeared itself to the hearts of whatever group he happened to be speaking to any particular moment.

The euphoria of the November 1996 victory was short-lived as the Administration returned to its sleepwalk, while the criminal investigation proceeded. Greg Albertson was left to clean up the mess; it was not until the following Spring that the new President realized he needed serious advice from the old President. By this he meant venerable Milton Buckminster Wallace Prescott.

# The Gathering Storm

Saturday, April 3, 1999 (9 a.m.)

THE FIRST HINTS OF SPRING were showing in the woodlands of the Catoctin Mountains as the motorcade proceeded to the main entrance at Camp David. Official Washington was running on a lower level of frantic anxiety with the departure of Congress the prior week for its Easter break. President Albertson had come up to the Maryland retreat the previous day. He needed time to relax, and also to prepare for his visitor. The meeting, although subject to the usual high level of security, was being downplayed. Nevertheless, former President Prescott was at the gate and the current President had every reason to feel that so were the wolves of history.

The limousine had barely halted when a rear door popped open and a trim, healthy 70ish gentleman emerged from the vehicle. He was sportily attired in fashionable deck shoes, natty blanco trousers, dark blue polo shirt, a tailored navy blazer, Ray Ban shades, and all topped off with a baseball cap emblazoned with the Presidential seal. This five foot seven, 150 pound grandfather appeared as if he were on his way to his favorite past-time—yachting. Milton Prescott was clearly enjoying his retirement, having long ago recovered from the fleeting disappointment of not being returned to that "darn gold fish bowl...and we made progress on what we believed we had as our goals...Martha sure had fun...the American people are guided in their wisdom."

Greg Albertson (a generation younger, a half-foot taller and thirty pounds heavier) always seemed in a formal pose, even on Casual Fridays. His detractors snickered he was the type of person who would have his blue jeans ironed by a valet before wearing them. Albertson was given this rejoinder by Mr. De Witt's head speechwriter: "Of course I don't do that! I'm a regular guy. I iron them myself." So, here he stood in the latest, best offerings in walking shoes, khaki slacks and pure cotton, salmon-toned polo shirt from J. Peterman. Hesitating a second the President stepped forward to shake hands with someone who could understand his troubles.

"Mr. President," one said.

"Mr. President," replied the other.

"Oh, enough formalities, Greg. Just call me Milt. How's the family?"

"Thanks...Milt...they're well. Tracy and the children are at our estate in Florida. They need to escape from the tension as much as I do," said Albertson.

"Ten-sion...sounds military," replied Prescott. "It fits...problems keep marching upon you in this job. Let's walk! It's too grand a morning to be admiring the carpet in the study."

The former President directed the incumbent towards a path that ran back into the property and away from the main buildings. Within a few minutes the men were far enough along the gravel-coated walkway that it would be easy for them to forget the ominous presence of the outside world. The trailing retinue of a double team of Secret Service Agents served as a reminder, however. A stirring breeze from the southwest carried with it the scents and sounds of the awakening season. A crystalline, azure heaven was the playground of a squadron of crows; in staccato harmony they declared their appreciation of the day.

"Did you have a good flight?" Albertson asked.

"Yes, Greg, I did. Thanks. Traffic wasn't too bad at Idelwild. Of course, it helps to have special clearance for immediate take-off...this is one thing I truly miss," Prescott sighed, gesturing at the forest-endowed landscape.

"Yes, Milt," replied the President, consciously making the effort this time to personalize his remarks, "I know what you mean. If I could telecommute, this would be an ideal location for a home office."

"The headlines are full of what you have to deal with," Prescott commiserated. "I'm thankful for the briefing summaries your people send out. Is it as wild as it seems?"

Albertson sighed. "From one week to the next it's difficult to know which trouble spot is going to be the one that blows up first. China, Mexico, Basraistan—and of all places, Canada! They're all in one mad rush for unwanted attention. My advisers are split every which way. They became so complacent in being able to judge topics by poll findings that now they're left flummoxed on issues lacking public consensus. Milt, I'm glad you could come. I need to speak with someone whose eyes don't glaze over because an issue doesn't involve a constituency group."

Prescott laughed. "Well, I've been accused of glazing and causing glazing."

The President stopped and asked directly, "Milt, what do you think of these situations? What can I do about them?"

The men had reached a clearing where a small pond nestled in a sun-washed corner of the woodland. A sturdy oak bench sat within easy pebble tossing distance of the shoreline. The former President pointed towards the scene saying, "Greg, let's sit for a while. I think our shadows need a rest."

They walked over and seated themselves while the attempting-to-be-unobtrusive Agents readjusted the protective cordon. Communication system static merged with bird song—the equivalent of a raspy cough in a hushed cathedral.

Scattered throughout the clearing were crowds of those muted aureate trumpeters of Spring; the former President removed his cap and sunglasses. His neatly trimmed gray hair was combed back, and his pale blue eyes swept the scene. "Where to begin…" Prescott muttered as he gathered his thoughts. Over the course of the next half hour Greg Albertson received more straightforward opinion than he had in the prior six months.

"The Soviet Republic of China," began Prescott. "I know China. Served there as Ambassador during Rocky's second term. That society seems older than time. Mao was their Stalin, the two unrestrained butchers of the 20th Century. Both dragged their nations into the modern era by chains. The Chairman probably killed more of his own folks than the enemy did in The Global War."

[What was initially a regional conflict evolved into The Global War with simultaneous hostilities on far-separated fronts. The earliest phase was ignited by the Nippon Empire's attack on China in 1932. It took on global characteristics in September 1941 when the People's Republics of Eurasia (PREA) launched conquering assaults against its Central Europe and Central Asia neighbors that had gained independence when the Czarist Empire ended in 1917. Stalin, in cruel irony, renamed Russia and the captive nations as the People's Republics of Eurasia. America became involved in Asia following the Battle of the South China Sea on November 25, 1941; this event saw U.S. forces block an attempted invasion of the Philippines by Nippon. The U.S. had for some time been able to decode Nippon's military communications through a system labeled MAGIC, and thus had warning of the planned invasion. In July 1942 Germany's fractious democratic government was further undermined by internal subversion. It was then coerced to accept a partition of the country into two nation-states. This was agreed to in order to forestall an outright invasion of Germany by the PREA. The U.S. in response sent troops to France to bolster the defenses of the Western European democracies. Warfare in Asia ceased in August 1943 with Nippon's surrender following America's unleashing of an atomic bomb against its forces on Okinawa.]

Prescott continued, "People were killed in the millions as well by Uncle Joe, he's believed to have ordered the murder of that German beer-hall fanatic in '33, and yet he never had to worry about an invader...the Global War, years of savagery. Some historians will tell you that if TR hadn't been so persuasive in 1914 and pushed for the Second Congress of Vienna the world might have faced an earlier world-wide conflict...Red Guards were bad news. China needs reform. Folks in the countryside consider themselves advanced if they have piped water and a connection for electricity. Tiananmen Square massacre won't stop people from wanting freedom. This year's the tenth anniversary. The democracy movement is now tied to the southern zone entrepreneurs. They need practical rule of law to do international business...property rights, copyrights, intellectual proprietary protection...it's as if they exist in different realities...political China, economic China...the business class and their emerging middle class don't care about socialist dogma...they have practical needs and want practical responses...Business wise they're top notch; they'll soon be the second largest economy—first, if we let them get by. That nation is facing a social earthquake. Can't retain strict controls on information, innovation, incentives and expect business to generate profits for the regime... one side will have to move...Beijing wins, it's a step back... the innovators win, then they get a great leap forward."

"The Republic of Taiwan...set up after liberation from the Nippon Empire...wanted nothing to do with the mainland- always separate society anyway. Now looks at the reformers as useful partners. Might consider some form of federation. Won't stand for being forced into anything."

"Other side of the country is looking to break away, Xinjiang Province. Moslem population. Wants connection to their brethren in central Asia."

"Beijing has two power points...the Army, the Politburo... the Army wants to keep its income from the factories it runs...Politburo thinks Mao is still a god, and that people will follow any directive if they put his name in it."

"The North Koreans are incensed at Beijing for allowing that high-level defector to travel on to Seoul. The Pyongyang junta believed China would always be its protector. It was China's troops that split the peninsula in 1944. The defector incident stirred up animosities from '50 when Mao blocked their invasion of the South. He feared Dewey would use the Big One when the Pacific Fleet's Western Task Force was sent into the Sea of Nippon."

The President interrupted this runaway train of thought by injecting, "What if the Chinese or the Koreans had called our bluff? The material I've seen on President Dewey's discussions with the National Security Council and the service Chiefs doesn't show a decisive plan. They seemed willing to draw a line, daring someone to cross it. But no mention of a nuclear option. How could they consider participating in a second conflict when U.S. forces were already in a fire-fight in the Balkans? We would have been engaged in simultaneous wars on two continents. I would oppose that even now."

Prescott gained a second wind and launched his reply. "Mao was undone by Stalin. Joe had no time for niceties. He showed his ruthlessness beginning with the 1930 coup that ousted the Kerensky government. When Joe tried to dump Yugoslavia's Tito in '50 by using renegade Serbian army officers the illusion of socialist solidarity was destroyed. The so-called volunteers who arrived from the East to help their Slav brothers liberate themselves from Tito's willingness to say *nyet* to the Kremlin showed the West that The People's Republics of Eurasia was just a cover for Russian imperialism. The fact that leftist rebels were also staging an uprising in Greece led to the Allied response. Overtly we sent aid to Athens, covertly military supplies moved across the Greek-Yugoslav frontier to bolster Tito's forces. Once the formal NATO structure came in place American troops served as cavalry units when the action got hot. That some of our guys wandered north and took out some of Stalin's goons was never publicly acknowledged. The Russians couldn't make a point of it because we would counter with revelations concerning his involvement. It suited everyone's agenda to remain mum."

[In March 1917 Russia's Czarist regime was ousted by a pro-democracy rebellion led by Alexander Kerensky. The nation's vast social and economic difficulties hampered the establishment of a strong democratic system. On May 7, 1930 the Marxist Party leader, Josef Stalin, led a violent coup that installed a brutal dictatorship.]

Prescott then remarked, "When the North Koreans decided to attempt to spread their wonderful system of depravation and repression, Dewey advised Mao through back channel communications that the U.S. wasn't going to waste resources swatting a fly such as Kim Il Sung. One shot would suffice. The Task Force ships were to give the impression of being the delivery system."

Albertson looked startled, and ran his fingers through his thinning dark hair. "Where did you get that background information?" he asked. "The official records I've seen contain no such details."

The former President laughed, and pronounced in his best snob-class hauteur, "Well, actually, old chap...you are in the wrong country club!" Chuckling at his own joke, Prescott continued, "Love that stiff upper lip bit, not me really. Martha says I'm a real cut up."

Albertson smiled wanly, uncertain if protocol permitted him to glare at a predecessor. "You were saying..." hoping to lead the discussion back on track.

Prescott saw the strained reaction on the President's face, shook his head, and began again. "When President

Rockefeller called me to the Oval Office in 1964 he advised me he was planning on establishing diplomatic relations with China. Rocky knew his opponent in November would be Senate Majority leader Lyndon Johnson; and, that Johnson would try labelling him as the standard-bearer of the war party. Johnson wanted to claim that Rocky was too anxious to use force, he wasn't to be trusted with the Bomb, that he'd leave us all pushing up daisies."

"Well," interjected the President, "your party did get us into two conflicts since the Global War even though we were not attacked. And one when Mr. Rockefeller was barely in office ten months. It was an open secret then concerning how close China was to exploding its first atomic device, despite the League of Nations' failure to find evidence of such plans. We were sharply rebuked by the League and the Organization of Western Hemisphere States (OWHS) in '61 for sending our troops to oust Castro." Holding up his hands to forestall a rebuttal the President added, "Yes, I realize Cuba is today a viable democracy, probably the most stable one in Latin America. However, there was no smoking gun showing Castro was linked to any foreign power. I know he mistreated some of his people, but we can't save every nation from misfortune."

Prescott replied, "Smoking gun means the bullet has been fired...that's what makes politics so exciting. Two groups evaluating the same issue from different perspectives and engaging in a vigorous debate. Rocky thought all those freighters from Eastern Europe docked in Havana might have been the source of Castro's development of a strategic missile system."

Laughing again to defuse the tension, Prescott continued, "Back to '64...The Yanks were in the Series that year, not again for a long time...played a little ball myself...met the Babe...met Dewey too at the Oval Office session with Rocky. He gave me all the background details not in the files. Tom had been a prosecutor, you know...felt he didn't have enough to indict (oops, sorry) the North Koreans in '50, so he kept the official files clean. The decision made was to show the flag, and let the world believe Mao stopped a war in Korea. Tom said the only person who was aware that he was holding the Bomb as a live option in the event of an invasion was his National Security Advisor, Dwight Eisenhower. Ike viewed a land conflict in East Asia as extremely difficult for us to fight."

"It must have been a factor in Dewey's reasoning for accepting and promoting the 1954 Geneva Accord on Indo-China," said Albertson.

"Yes, it was," replied Prescott. "Unfortunately, Ike's point was proven by our involvement in the Philippines. Twelve years, 50 thousand plus casualties, indecisive outcome, tragedy....VietNam, the information the Dewey Administration obtained from ground sources in Southeast Asia was that Ho Chi Minh could honestly win a free election. The only ones pushing to reject the accord were the French; yet, they had no platform for supporting their objective of re-establishing a colonial regime following the Dienbienphu catastrophe. We had suffered considerable human and material costs between 1941 and 1951 trying to make the world safe for democracy. What were we to do? Send an army of our boys to trample around a jungle for who knows how long attempting to prop up a non-indigenous regime?"

"And, no...Mr. Dewey did not contemplate the Bomb then. Korea is next door to Japan and sits on a crossroads with China and Russia. He could see a sense of geopolitical interest. Viet Nam? Stop any of our citizens today on the street, ask them what it is, where it is, unless they're a CEO of a sports shoe manufacturing firm, wouldn't know, wouldn't care."

Looking to patch together this kaleidoscopic discussion, the President inquired, "What can I expect from the Chinese leaders over the next 18 months?"

"Caution," Prescott returned in an uncharacteristically

succinct manner. "They know their grip is tenuous. They'll wait for an opening gambit, expecting it to be an appeal from Hong Kong for true home rule. The democracy movement wants to show that it is Chinese, revolutionary, but still directed toward reform. There's been talk of a long march from Hong Kong to Beijing with the theme of 'A New Constitution For A New Century.'"

"Speaking of marches," added the President, "What about Mexico? The daily rallies in the capital are getting more extensive every week."

Milton Prescott stood at this point. "Greg, speaking of walking, I need to stretch. If you rest you rust at my age."

"You look great ..."

"...for a geezer! Ha! Don't look so serious. Martha calls me that all the time. Still better than most of the fellas at the club. Speed boating, few rounds of golf each week. Might try another jump this Summer."

"A what?"

"Parachuting. Haven't done it since my days in the OSS. Legs get stiff if I dawdle." The former President waved towards the Agents, indicating they were moving on. Men talked into their sleeves or coat collars, and a helicopter came overhead, proceeding in the intended direction.

[OSS—The Office of Strategic Services is the U.S. spy agency.]

"Reminds me of Eastern Europe in '89," starting in midstream Prescott renewed his comments, switching to America's southern neighbor. "The patient is dead, yet everyone's too polite to announce the diagnosis. Their former ruling clique is still in denial about losing their last Presidential election. The current Government controls a shrinking area around the country. Their southern States are in various stages of revolt, and many Governors are on the payroll of either a local warlord or the Durango narcotics cartel. The former dominant political group, the Popular Revolutionary Movement, never trusted the voters to choose them in an open contest."

[The Popular Revolutionary Movement is often referred to by the initials for its name in Spanish—MPR. The organization totally controlled Mexican politics for over 80 years.]

"Six years ago they got sloppy, didn't think they needed the usual pressure tactics, that everyone would be like sheep and just follow along. The main opposition surprised them, put up a joint candidate and a strong campaign. Won for the first time ever. However, the MPR still controlled their Congress. Now with Mexico's economic survival at stake, the MPR is back to its old format and making matters worse. Refugees here could present a significant challenge. Do we use force to seal the border, protecting our communities from a social tsunami? If we do, does the pressure inevitably build up within Mexico generating an explosion sooner rather than later, confronting us with a flood of desperate people anyway? It's hard to offer the Mexicans advice. They have reasons for distrusting us."

"Yes, indeed," said the President. "I had lunch with the Ambassador lately. Any suggestion was received very stiffly. They almost suspect we engineered their problems in retaliation for the drug trafficking headquartered in their country. They say we created the cartel by our own weakness, made the dealers stronger with our money, then accuse their hard-pressed government of failing to eradicate the problem."

Milton Prescott nodded in agreement. "We could see Mexico fracture similar to India in 1993. Sectarian violence broke India into a handful of nation-states, antagonistic towards each other, set against a backdrop of an abundance of unaccounted-for weapons."

The two men had reached the edge of the tree-line and descended a slope towards a pasture, through which a small creek flowed. Prescott continued his remarks, "Basraistan... we created a mirage in the sand. Its only asset is oil, its greatest liability is people. No one there is truly satisfied with our map drawing. Iran and Iraq made smaller, but still have big ambitions to control the region. Basraistan was to be a safe home for the Shias; but some Sunnis remained, and their brethren in Baghdad want to 'save' them from what they see as foreign occupation forces. We have 10,000 troops there, far less than the Pentagon wanted, trying to keep the peace among folks who can't live together and won't live apart."

Greg Albertson stated, "Canada has its own concerns about possible dissolution. There's a referendum scheduled for December of next year in Quebec. The Parti Kebec is again promoting independence for the Province. However, the rising power up North—the Populist Party—opposes any special deal or separation for Quebec."

"Well," said the former President. "I have more insider trading information for you."

"Did you ever truly leave the OSS?" Albertson laughingly asked.

"The order of Melchizedek...DDO for Black Thorn... stories for another day...my youngest son, Jed, as you know is Governor of Illinois. My predecessor, Michael Morrison, held the post before coming to Washington. He'll be rated as one of the great ones...surprised everyone...former sports announcer emerges as President, good talker, what can he do? Just negotiates the first-ever actual reduction in strategic nuclear arsenals. Pushes back the hands of the doomsday clock. The world doesn't want any more Okinawas. One atomic attack is enough for all human history. Not many know how close we came in the '75 Berlin crisis to nuclear war. The Great Communicator, likes horses, recommended Montana to my son as a vacation spot..."

[In October 1975 President John Kennedy was faced with the possibility of a war with the PREA when the Marxist regime of East Germany shot down a U.S. cargo plane traveling to West Berlin.]

"You were speaking about Canada..." interjected Albertson hopefully.

"Getting there." smiled Prescott. "Jed met the Premier of one of the western Canadian Provinces in Montana. Were talking late one night. The Premier pops out a question, 'How does one join America?' My son figured he meant citizenship. The PM meant Statehood. Would not say it directly, but if Quebec goes loose we may need more stars."

The President grabbed his companion's arm, turning him so they were face to face. "Never repeat that! Call your son and swear him to secrecy! Did he relate the conversation to anyone else? If the world thought we might tamper..."

"No, no!" the former President assured him. "Jed knows better. Actually, the Premier pleaded with him the next day to forget what he said. Blamed it on a long ride and Molson."

"Let's sit again," said Albertson, pointing to another bench. "My knees need to recover...You've given me a lot to consider. What do I do with it?"

Prescott reflected momentarily, then replied. "On China, let them know we're not interfering; however, another bloody crackdown is unacceptable. Can't hide behind business leaders who dream of easy profits. Can't be in the family of nations if they want to react like savages. Keep emphasizing that political and economic reforms go hand-in-hand. Be polite but specific. From experience I know the consequences of vague signals. If the leadership's loyalty is to China, not personal power, they will allow the people a public voice. If the rulers block reform, it doesn't end the desire for reform. There's a proverb concerning a drip of water eventually breaking the strongest rock. Democracy is the water. Totalitarianism is the rock."

"Mexico is the same yet different. The government is shaky but pro-democracy. The opposition wants a restoration of their autocratic rule. Real question is the intention of the drug cartel. Will they remain satisfied with being criminals, or do they see themselves using the national economy to launder their profits from addicts? We need to stay behind the scenes, yet make the politicians on both sides aware of our preparedness to help. Got to push the message in our schools that drugs kill. Addiction is not recreational. Stop the drugs, stop the corruption, stop the cartel."

"Canada should know that tribalization is not the way forward. Breaking up in anger accelerates ethnic conflicts. Look at West Asia. Do they want to go the way of the societies there with clan members stalking members of other clans with guns and bombs? The Anglo and Franco Canadians may never initiate hostilities, nevertheless two or more carved-out States won't alleviate underlying contentions. NAFTA could be harmed. Outside referees could be the best option. The English and French Premiers could relate how their nations renounced centuries of animosity and are now partners in the European Federation. With these scenarios, north and south, we have to work on having the right people in the same room together. They need to be shaking hands with each other, not shaking fists at each…"

Behind them a commotion arose. An all-terrain vehicle had pulled up sharply to the Secret Service Agents' mini-camp. The President's Chief of Staff exited the Humvee, and ran down the incline.

"What's this about?" Albertson muttered to himself. As his aide neared, he repeated his question aloud adding, "Catch your breath. Why didn't you call?"

"The Detail said your order was no interruption, unless there was an act of war," the C-O-S wheezed. The man looked at the former President, hesitating.

"Talk already!" Albertson snapped. "I think we can trust this guy!"

The C-O-S inhaled deeply to calm himself, then broke the news. "There's been an explosion in Beijing, nearly an hour ago. It's Saturday night there. A truck containing what is believed to have been a large fertilizer and fuel bomb crashed into the motorcade of the Chinese President, Jiang Zemin. Dozens of people are dead, including Jiang. The Army has sent thousands of additional troops into the capital. They're detaining all foreigners found on the street—including journalists. World Network News' correspondent was on the air, live, when an armored personnel carrier pulled up, soldiers poured out, seized her and halted transmission. Our Embassy states they see tanks not too far from their front door."

"What about our operatives within the Forbidden City? Any word from them?" the President inquired.

"We've had just one short message. They don't believe it's an inside job. Too many people are fat and happy with the current...er...prior arrangement."

Prescott asked, "No signs of an attempt by the military? They reacted without much delay."

"None that we know of," answered the C-O-S. "Gentlemen, let's return to the main house. The link to the Situation Room is ready."

The three men rapidly walked up to the top of the slope, entered the waiting vehicle and sped off to obtain details on the world's latest act of madness. When they arrived at the entrance of the lodge, Vice President Ann Linus was waiting.

Ms. Linus had been a Representative from Wyoming who deftly employed her typical middle class appearance and style to promote an assertive agenda of women's issues. The definition of "women's issues" changed over the course of her 12 terms in the House. Initially, the appropriateness of a woman in politics was a central topic; eventually the Beltway establishment understood that women's issues are issues of personal concern to over 50% of enrolled voters— so attention began to be paid.

When Greg Albertson, new to his promotion to the West Wing, inquired if she would be interested in his previous job, Ann Linus accepted after a few moments of decent hesitation. "The glass ceiling's been pushed up another notch" is how she explained her intention of re-charging a profession she had grown tired of for protecting the "static-quo."

As the vehicle's doors were opened by Agents now displaying automatic weapons, the Vice President stepped up to Mr. Albertson and quietly informed him, "The Chairman of the Joint Chiefs is on the video phone. He is one tense Marine. He needs to talk to you pronto!"

The group went inside and directly to the communications room. Albertson seated himself at a large desk where a TV-phone monitor was situated. "General, what can you tell me?"

The Chairman, Four Star General Cory Stratton of the U.S. Marine Corps, looked every bit the Hollywood image of a "hard as a reinforced bunker" style professional warrior. Stratton stood 6 feet 2 inches tall, weighed an athletically fit 210 pounds, had close-cropped dark hair, and ebony eyes which reflected either his private impish playfulness or a public sternness that warned that nothing less than maximum performance would be tolerated. Within his full-time duties he had set aside the hours needed to acquire his Doctorate in International Diplomacy.

Colleagues still marvelled at the tale of Stratton's neutralizing an enemy intruder at Alliance HQ in Dubai during the Persian Gulf War. An Iranian commando had penetrated all the base's security levels, finally barging into the room where the General was conducting a staff meeting. Two seconds later the intruder was dead, shot in the forehead by Stratton, who apologized for the interruption then continued the meeting. Stratton was the commanding field officer for the international alliance assembled by President Prescott in response to Iran's invasion of Iraq and Kuwait in July 1990. Stratton was named as Chairman of the Joint Chiefs of Staff by President Jeffrey De Witt in 1995.

"Mr. President, the activity in Beijing may be a diversion," the Chairman reported sternly. Several exclamations of "What!" arose from behind the President. Albertson added his own inquiry. "What more is happening?"

General Stratton laid out the facts in cold directness. "The North Koreans are providing mounting evidence of going on a war footing. They have sent aloft far more than their usual contingent of aircraft; from what we know of their fuel supply levels they don't have the resources to waste on night patrols when they lack the proper equipment. Their divisions along the frontier have apparently risen to a higher level of alert. Their propaganda broadcasts alternate between warning the Seoul Government against adventurism, and calling upon the people of the South to join their Northern cousins in a crusade to oust the oppressors of Korea."

The President paused as he started to speak. Finally, he asked, "Do we have anything concrete? Were reserves moved up? Did the front line troops approach the DMZ? Perhaps they're only jittery following the events in China."

Stratton replied, "We had reports last week of deliveries by rail to forward positions of heavy-weight ordnance. It wasn't activated or brought into the field straight away. They seem to be playing a shell game. Probably figured we were watching from overhead."

"So where is it? How much or how many of whatever was there? Was it tanks, artillery, attack helicopters?"

"Sir, we don't know the answer to any of those questions. Funding for HUMINT was deprioritized in the past several budgets...excuse me for a moment, Sir...Yes, Colonel." General Stratton moved away to converse with an aide who had approached with a report. If it was possible, Stratton seemed more grim-faced when he sat back before the phone. "I have been handed an update regarding Korea. There is a considerable concentration of North Korean aircraft moving south bound over the Yellow Sea. The craft took off from airfields near Pyongyang, headed for the coast and have been flying at low level with their lights on, but below their own radar's capacity to track. We have them under surveillance by two AWACS. The propaganda broadcasts are openly accusing the South of having sent raiding parties across the DMZ."

"Have any ROK forces taken such actions?" Albertson inquired.

"No, Sir, Mr. President," answered Stratton. "But Seoul high command is ready to initiate action if anyone so much as whispers 'advance.' Sir, we are getting a running commentary based on the observations by the AWACS and satellite positioning updates. If someone at your site will switch the reception to the wide-screen monitor, you can observe the activities board."

A technician with the President made the necessary adjustment. The video link-up was projected onto a wall-size screen. Before them the group could see the activity in the White House Situation Room. A computer-generated map displayed the constantly updated placement of aircraft, ships and land-based military units in and around the frontier area of the two Koreas. An off-screen voice provided commentary:

"The NKAF heavy squadron continues to proceed south along the western coast, about one mile offshore. There has been a noticeable increase in motor vehicle activity in-land of the coast just above the DMZ. Early indications are they may be deploying a SAM unit. This would be consistent with their allegations that ROK aircraft are attempting to challenge the sovereignty of the North's airspace."

"Mr. President." It was General Stratton overriding the commentary. "As you can see on the board, no Republic of Korea or U.S. aircraft are within five miles of the DMZ. Pyongyang Radio has been rattling off a series of accusations. We are observing, but not doing anything provocative."

"Thank you, General," said the President. The commentary resumed, "...continuing their course. In two minutes the squadron will be adjacent to the frontier. A ROK Aegis-class destroyer, as projected, is sitting on the edge of the five-mile buffer. The squadron is altering direction and altitude, coming in-land over their own territory. They are at 1000 feet, crossing the coast...ALERT! On-shore radar has lit up...aircraft climbing and accelerating, continuing northward...increased radio traffic...NK border security seems not aware of squadron's status as one of their own...squadron is not responding to calls to identify...they were silent on the way south...warnings being issued...radar seeking to lock-onto the squadron...LAUNCH! Indications from suspected SAM site of multiple releases...craft heading back over the sea, evading projectiles...LAUNCH! Numerous...AWACS report possible dozen large projectiles launched...trajectory is away from, repeat AWAY FROM, location of squadron... projectiles are climbing, arching over the DMZ...ROK aircraft are firing counter-launches at projectiles, some are targeting the SAM site...ALERT! Projectiles are down-sloping above city of Inchon........

WHAT!?? OH, Nooo...AIR-BURST! STRONG THERMAL FLASH!! We're getting interruptions from primary AWAC...MUSHROOM CLOUD BEING REPORTED!!!...air and ground sources verify..."

"STRATTON!! GENERAL STRATTON!! What in hell is going on!" the President was standing and screaming at the screen. Stratton appeared, held up one hand, indicated 'wait.' Minutes later, seemingly an eternity, he reappeared. "Mr. President," in a voice held authoritatively calm, the Chairman addressed the bewildered gathering at Camp David. "There has been a likely nuclear strike against Inchon. The second launch is believed to have been a series of Scuds. Obviously one contained an extreme warhead. By our standards it was a small device. However, damage on the ground will be considerable. The Seoul Government is demanding that we initiate an immediate retaliatory strike, and one which will be beyond mere response in kind. Several of their squadrons have already engaged Northern ground troops, and destroyed NKAF fighters, radar sites and the SAM unit that launched the attack. Fortunately, no North Korean ground forces have advanced towards the DMZ. At this point we cannot state with assurance that this was a deliberate act by the North. If this wasn't an orchestrated scenario we have a possibility of either a rouge local commander, or one who didn't know the squadron was one of his own. When the jets crossed in-land the SAM commander may have panicked thinking there really was an invasion, and let loose with his big gun."

"How is that possible?" demanded Albertson. "Isn't North Korea buttoned-up so tight you need permission to sneeze? What is a nuclear weapon doing in the hands of a glorified artillery officer?"

"Well..." A voice from behind the President began. It was Milton Prescott. "If you remember those NSC intel reports on the status of control in the Hermit Kingdom, matters have been slipping since Kim Jong-il inherited his father's titles. He's never achieved a consensus among the elite. The military has been suffering from the imploding economy along with everyone else. It's become a laissez-faire dictatorship. Someone along the chain of command may have stepped up, and overstepped us into a disaster."

"Oh...yes...those reports," Albertson said, more to himself than aloud. Recovering, he asked his almost forgotten guest, "Could they be so stupid to do this deliberately?"

"We've never held to our announced plans for sanctions. They probably saw us as no threat to their ambitions. However, their ambitions are guided by fear and paranoia. So your guess is as good as mine," replied Prescott.

"Mr. President," the Chairman interjected.

Two people replied "Yes." One added, "Oops, it's for you."

"Mr. President," General Stratton began again. "I have the South Korean Defense Minister on the line. He's waiting for your authorization to initiate a joint deep counter-strike. They are willing to go it alone, if you request so."

"NO! NO!! ", Albertson screamed as he pounded the desk top. "They cannot do that! Are they all insane? If any retaliation is struck it will never stop at being 'surgical.' We'll end up with a full-scale conflict on the peninsula, one with a nuclear component. Moreover, we still don't know the background. How many more warheads do they have?"

The Chairman first replied to someone off-screen. "Sec State heard him! She's going to have to talk them off the ledge!...Excuse me, Sir. In response to your question, Mr. President, we don't have the resources to ascertain their capabilities in this field. The agreement the North signed in '94 was intended to halt their development program. The inspection program the League of Nations was to carry out became non-functional with all the concessions made to satisfy the North's complaints. National policy proscribed inserting any of our personnel in a stealth capacity."

"What are they broadcasting now?"

"Local music. When the fire-fight began the station went silent. Then returned without comment."

The President paced the room, clenching and unclenching his fists. Finally, he spoke. "General, order all our forces to stand down."

"The AWACS?" asked Stratton.

"Oh...er...no. No. Leave them up. However, no offensive aircraft is to be near the DMZ. Pull them back or keep them on the tarmac. No ground patrols. Don't we have electronic monitors in place?"

"Yes, however..."

"Rely on those for now. Also, it is imperative that no, I repeat NO, ROK unit, aircraft or vessel take any action. We must remember China has nukes and throw capacities far greater than Scuds. If we try slapping North Korea for this... incident, Seoul and perhaps Tokyo could be the next target; and, this time there wouldn't be any doubt of the intention. China will not accept any transgression into what it regards as its sphere of influence. Is the Secretary of State available?"

The Secretary came on-screen a few minutes later. "Mr. President, our Korean allies are vehemently incensed at our inaction. Their Defense Minister had to be physically restrained from entering our Embassy because he was in such a violent mood. Tragically, there is something to preoccupy their government for a while. They will come back soon looking for a better answer."

"Thank you for your viewpoint, Madame Secretary,"

replied the President. "I need you to persuade the Koreans personally of the wisdom of restraint. Please arrange for an immediate trip to Seoul. This will assure them of America's commitment. Secondly, try to contact someone, anyone, in Pyongyang who can give us information." With that said, he ended the link-up. President Albertson turned and faced the others. No one spoke.

Milton Prescott hopped off the stool he had been sitting upon, looked at his wrist watch and commented, "Will you look at the time. I thought hours had gone by. Perhaps we should return to 1600."

Amid the gathering crowd of aides, Secret Service Agents and military personnel, Greg Albertson stood as a man very much alone. His own was not the only government he seemed to have little control over.

# April's Aftermath

THE EVENTS OF APRIL 1999 brought into sharp focus the harsh reality that although the Armageddon-provoking tensions of the Proxy War era were gone, the world was still a particularly dangerous place.

[The Proxy War era, 1949 to 1991, refers to conflicts in the Balkans, the Philippines, Central America and the Caribbean between indigenous forces supported by the U.S. versus insurgents supported either by the People's Republics of Eurasia or by Soviet China. The U.S. also conducted covert action against these two adversaries in Central Asia. An American supported pro-democracy group overthrew Cuba's Marxist dictatorship in 1961. The Proxy War era is seen as ending when civilian demonstrations in Moscow led to a revolt which toppled the dictatorship of the PREA. China remains a totalitarian state, but 'Soviet' in name only.]

Some of the details of these tragedies were described in a White Paper generated by the Commission on the East Asia Incidents (as the events were officially labelled by the Administration), which was appointed by President Albertson a week after the assassination and the decimation of Inchon. The Commission's report was a dutiful recitation of facts already in the public domain through hard-news presentations by the dwindling number of media outlets that still pursued hard-news. The Commission also wrote a limited distribution addendum dealing with the more sensitive material.

The events were in deed connected. No memo, audio or video tape was ever uncovered; yet, enough circumstantial evidence was obtained to show North Korean complicity in the murder of China's President, and to confirm allegations that the assassination was to serve as cover for the outbreak of war in Korea. Unofficial and unprecedented co-operation between the intelligence agencies of China, South Korea, Japan and the United States revealed a conspiracy fathered by Kim Jong-il. He sought to bolster his collapsing regime by counteracting what he considered was a plot by Beijing and Seoul to undermine him. The North's sole nuclear warhead (closer to being a hyper-augmented 'dirty bomb' than the devices poised on top of the multitude of ICBMs planted around the globe) was deliberately aimed at Inchon. An estimated 2.5% of the city's population of 2.8 million people would eventually die from either blast effects or radiation poisoning. In theory, the populace of the South was to blame the Seoul Government; they would revolt, overthrow the regime and happily invite Kim to be the Dear Leader of a reunited peninsula. What the dictator got for his trouble was a choice from the head of his own internal security apparatus of suicide or execution. A few weeks after the attacks a brief statement on Pyongyang Radio advised the people that Kim was dedicating his time to a special project related to the nation's food supply. Before the end of the year another brief report announced that Kim had died following a short illness. No public or private funeral or memorial service was held. He was effectively erased from official memory. A Council of State, comprised of the leaders of the Party, the Army and the security agency, took control of the country.

The United States agreed to establish a relief fund totalling $114 billion to compensate the families of those who died or were injured, and to aid in decontaminating and rebuilding the city of Inchon.

The death of Jiang Zemin left China in a short-term power vacuum. Once the authorities reassured themselves that their grip on power was not endangered by an array of foreign enemies they settled into complacency. The democracy movement restrained itself from public demonstrations, if only for self-protection. Besides the new communication format—the Internet—was beginning to work its way into the country behind the façade of business operations.

In the United States the initial relief at having avoided a possibly nuclear conflict soon gave way to an alternative analysis. America's talk-radio gab-meisters began nagging at their loyal legions of listeners that the USA had been denied a victory once again by wimpy inside-the-Beltway politicos. All the well-chewed over views of how the U.S. tank forces had been restrained during the Persian Gulf War, and denied the glory of rolling into Tehran, were brought out again. In April, the American public was told, we had the opportunity to topple the NK Reds; our gallant allies in the South were well prepared to advance and put an end to the brutes up North. They simply needed U.S. air cover, a few cruise missiles strikes, one or two B-52 raids, and they would provide all the on-site ground forces. In a short time Southern troops would roll up to the Yalu River and all Korea would be free. Did this happen? NO! WHY NOT? Because the unelected occupant of the Executive Mansion would not listen to the advice of the Pentagon, and refused to act. Despite rebuttals by the White House and the Defense Department that no U.S. military officer ever suggested a move against the North, the accusation kept running ahead of the denial. The mini-wild fire of public agitation was ready to burn out when a news release re-ignited it. In August, the Chairman of the Joint Chiefs, Cory Stratton, announced he would not seek reappointment to the post. He had already served the standard maximum of two 2-year terms; while an additional term was not prohibited, it would be very unusual. Despite statements from the White House, the Defense Department and General Stratton that he originally notified the President as far back as January of this intention, the rumor that Stratton was quitting because he was appalled by Albertson's behavior kept running ahead of the denial.

General Stratton indicated his departure was based solely on his desire to spend more time with his wife and children. It would also provide him the time to complete his autobiography, 'American Sojourn'. This would relate his family's history from his grandparents' involvement in the self-rule movement of their homeland (the Cayman Islands) at the beginning of the Century, to his parents' emigration to the United States after the Stratton family was invited to leave by the British colonial administration in 1937 (Stratton's father had taken up the leadership of the cause), to his own birth in Brooklyn in 1941, and his life and times as an American of Caribbean heritage.

# *Destiny Interrupted*

"It's why they play the game." This oft-quoted remark by America's most famous football coach is used as a cautionary tale-in-brief that the inevitable isn't always so.

Cory Stratton's book-signing tour in the Autumn and early Winter of 1999 took on all the characteristics of a Presidential campaign. The perceived wisdom was there seemed little left to decide but the style of drapes to be chosen for the Oval Office following former General Stratton's assured election victory.

And then all that could have happened did not. The final stop on Stratton's tour was to be in the Borders mega-book store in Brooklyn. However, the event was cancelled in a brief press release: "Due to an illness in the family General Stratton will be unable to attend the scheduled event at Borders. He will not be making any further public appearances this year."

One of the Stratton children died a few months later of sickle cell anemia.

# *Interregnum*

THE FIRST PRESIDENTIAL ELECTION of the new Millennium bore the scars of the public's disgust with politics-as-usual. After all the shouting was over the turnout was one of the lowest on record, 46%. Voters were asked to choose between the major party candidates who were both viewed as accidental nominees.

Greg Albertson obtained the Libertarian Party nomination by default. Various commentators speculated any one of four or five senior elected officials could have taken away the designation; but they all precluded a run for an assortment of thinly-veiled reasons. Actually, no senior official in the party thought any Libertarian candidate could win, given the events of the past several years.

That Albertson was elected to his own term as President was attributed directly to the Federalist Party candidate, Wallace Prescott—the eldest son of the former President. In the run-up to the 2000 election cycle it had been believed that former President Prescott's second son, Jedediah (or more usually, Jed) was a shoo-in for the Federalist Party nomination. However, the family's code of procedure intervened. While the Prescott clan was gathered at their residential compound along Maine's north coast, the incumbent politicians in attendance met for a discussion.

Jed was a two-term Governor of Illinois; and Wallace ("Wally") was just completing his third year as a U.S. Senator from Maine. The brothers had idly discussed on previous occasions Jed's seeking the Presidency. On the night after Christmas they met again to discuss the topic. Jed's concept of family loyalty imbued within him a sense of deference to his senior sibling. This necessitated posing a question he would deeply regret.

"Wally, you know all this talk about next year is getting serious."

"That's your problem, Jed. You're always looking on the serious side. Staff worries about serious. As leaders we just need to project a sense of calm."

"Being President is extremely serious business."

"Yeah, but there's all the more staff to handle the gritty details."

"You know my name has come up..."

"Ain't that a hoot? We'd be like the Adams family. Father and son Presidents. I wouldn't mind that."

"Oh...do you mean you have thought of yourself..."

"Some of my chums at the polo club said I'd be dandy! They said it would be a snap raising $100 million for the campaign."

Jed felt cold despite the room's warmth. "Oh...but...are you certain? It's very demanding..."

"You know what kiddo! I'm going to do it! Yes! I'm going to do it! Let's go tell Mom and Dad! Won't they be surprised?"

Jed sat in stunned silence for several minutes. Mom smiled thinly, while Dad pondered if he could persuade/coerce Wallace to accept the right people for his staff.

The formal campaign began in September 2000, following a non-eventful primary election process and even duller conventions. Greg Albertson and Wallace Prescott faced only nominal challenges; most of the nation spent the Spring and Summer not noticing either one.

The final round was also drawing minimal attention, until the weekend before Halloween. The Prescott family had gathered once again at its Maine homestead for a strategy conference on the closing days of the campaign. Wallace handed off an afternoon meeting to his chief of staff. Wally's interest centered on his new SUV which he wanted to test drive.

By 6 PM on that last Saturday in October breaking news reports were detailing the injuries Wallace Prescott had received when his SUV overturned as he cut too sharp a turn on a dirt road. A family spokesperson tried vainly for a few hours to cast doubt on who was driving at the time of the accident. The media reports included references, and video on several web-sites, of Wallace's frat-boy adventures while attending his father's Alma Mater.

Greg Albertson won the election by five Electoral Votes, and a popular vote margin of slightly more than 400,000. Wallace Prescott's failure to carry his home State provided Albertson with the margin of victory.

\* \* \* \* \*

Albertson's next four years in office were symbolized by his repeated use of the Presidential veto. The Federalists had maintained a narrow majority in the Senate after the 2000 election, while losing their majority in the House of Representatives. When they could not find the votes to override a veto the Federalists halted or delayed operations through filibusters. The opposing forces in Washington were often deadlocked. Domestic and foreign policy limped along in compromises of non-change. The only highlight in this period was the July 20, 2004 celebration of the 20th anniversary of the establishment on Sentinella of the permanent U.S. lunar base, Athena.

[In this history Terra's lunar companion is named Sentinella. It is said the name was first proposed by Leonardo da Vinci. In post-colonial American folklore Sentinella became St. Al (or simply "Al") as settlers moved westward. The moon was a beacon the people could relate to in the vast darkness of the inner continent's night.]

\* \* \* \* \*

While the United States was still grappling with the morass of Basraistan, Russia was being seized by an intractable conflict of its own. The legacy of the Czarist Empire and the People's Republics of Eurasia still lingered in the Caucasus and Central Asia. Russian troops and business arrangements kept the various regimes either off-balance or in a state of dependency. An insurgency borne of America's anti-Marxist campaign there in the 1960s had smouldered over the past decade. The Gulf War had a curious affect on a segment of the population. They saw the triumph of the Alliance over Iran as an affront to their fundamentalist based beliefs. The infidels, rather than Arab legions, had defeated the neo-Persians. The ruling family in Saudi Arabia, with some knowledge of the fanaticism of this faction, had barred the Alliance from using its territory during the Gulf War. Iran's gross mismanagement of troop and supply logistics had saved the Saudis from being overrun; Iran also chose to believe the Allied tank and infantry forces in Jordan and air forces in the Gulf States were only for show. Seven months after their invasion the Iranian forces were decimated.

Russia, because of its proximity to West Asia, became the focal point of attacks to avenge the honor of the true believers. While purporting to be the most loyal adherers to the dominant theology of the region, many scholarly observers debated otherwise concerning the fanatics. Waves of bombings and assassinations left a trail of horror that reached Moscow and St. Petersburg.

The movement's own web-site and videos identified its leader. He advocated uniting a disparate populous across Asia and Africa within a grandiose theocracy, Qaedaistan.

He was widely known by his *nom de guerre*, Abdul bin al-Quds. The movement was often referred to as al-Qaeda.

Propaganda became a weapon for al-Quds. In several videos and in-person interviews he berated Western leaders as a demonic plague threatening the true believers. He denigrated Russian officials as barbaric servants of the West who had betrayed their Asiatic heritage.

The destruction of St. Petersburg's City Hall on Orthodox Easter Sunday (April 15, 2001) ignited an obsession within the Moscow government to terminate al-Quds. More than 200 emergency service personnel were killed when a second set of explosives ripped through the City Hall structure causing it to collapse. Months of bribery, torture and executions (sometimes of entire families) led an elite brigade of Russian troops to a village a few miles south of Grozny, Chechnya. Approximately 375 people lived in the village, more than half of them being women and children. Less than a dozen survivors were found after the brigade swept the area with incendiary shells fired from mortars. One of the survivors was Abdul bin al-Quds.

Russia has never offered any public announcement of al-Quds' capture, or the related subsequent events. He was quickly put on a military transport plane to be brought to Moscow for interrogation and eventual execution. One hundred of Russia's best anti-insurgency troops accompanied al-Quds on the flight. As the plane, with an escort of fighter jets, was nearly landed at a military airfield near the capital, it was struck by a missile. The pilot had no opportunity to take evasive action, or to deploy counter-measures. The plane lost its tail section, cart wheeled in the air, then slammed into the field's tower. Over 300 people were killed, including al-Quds. The date was September 11, 2001.

\* \* \* \* \*

The Albertson Administration stumbled along through its term. Within its senior staff was a growing divide between those willing to accommodate the Federalist-controlled Senate, and those advocating a forceful challenge.

Matters came to a head when Vice President Ann Linus took the internal debate public in the Spring of 2003. At a generic meet-and-greet session of home State supporters the Vice President alluded to her possible Presidential candidacy in the following year. "I want to lead a party that cares enough about the American people to willingly take on entrenched attitudes and policy modes that don't work," said Ms Linus. She went a step farther. "My opinions are well known to our party's hierarchy. To them it seems my beliefs are an inconvenient truth they won't accept and can't refute."

These brave remarks, however, effectively ended any chance she had for the nomination. Ms Linus had never been accepted by the inner circle because she would not abandon her independent views. The party organization pushed through the candidacy of Pennsylvania's Governor Edward Galway.

The following year's political showdown was a confrontation pitting Galway (a veteran of the Gulf War, who now advocated decreased military involvement) and Senate Majority Leader Conrad Mitcher (a lacklustre Beltway insider). Galway's commitment to withdraw all U.S. troops from Basraistan was the key debate point between the candidates.

American forces were subjected to on-going bursts of casualties as the opposing social groups in Basraistan wallowed in manic fratricide. Galway bluntly summarized his position as "If those people want to waste a generation of their young adults while tearing the country apart, we shouldn't waste a generation of our young adults trying to hold that nation together."

A surge of battle deaths in October 2004 provided Galway with the momentum he needed for victory, obtaining 52% of the popular vote and a 90-vote Electoral College margin.

The opening sentence in Edward Galway's Inaugural Address on January 20, 2005 was, "All American military personnel will be out of Basraistan by this year's Fourth of July!" His supporters were ecstatic; the Joint Chiefs of Staff were confounded. They had anticipated that President Galway would proceed with his oft-stated pledge to redeploy the troops; yet they had in mind a phased withdrawal over 18 to 24 months. Now they had to evacuate more than 10,000 troops and support personnel—plus thousands of tons of equipment—in less than six months amid an increasingly hostile environment.

During the Fall campaign Senator Mitcher had remarked, in reply to a question at one of the televised debates, "Allies are countries that support the U.S. when they need help, and ignore the U.S. when we need help." Governor Galway had criticized the Senator's bluntness; by late February President Galway was acknowledging the Senator's accuracy. Of the several West Asia nations officially considered American allies only Israel and The Cyprus Confederation offered assistance in the redeployment.

Considerable use was also made of the Republic of Britain's air base on Diego Garcia, in the Indian Ocean. As the deadline grew closer the violence against the American troops actually increased. Both factions launched guerrilla and suicide assaults, one out of hope of what it could gain, the other out of fear of what it could lose. A catastrophic blow on May 23 ignited what became known as The Six Weeks' War. A troop ship carrying 1351 Marines and crew was departing that night under cover of darkness. Within minutes of leaving its berth the vessel was a flaming death trap. All on board were killed. Military officials believe improvised mines exploded next to the ship, and that the blasts ignited the munitions on-board.

The U.S. was required to stage round-the-clock air and missile strikes, to protect the remaining troops, in a ten-mile radius "red zone" that encircled the city of Al-Faw, the port in Basraistan being used as the final evacuation site.

*****

President Galway's withdrawal deadline was met two days early. The last American forces to leave Basraistan were a Delta Force contingent. Shortly after sunrise on July 2nd synchronized explosions devastated the on-shore facilities and harbor of Al-Faw. The waterway and docks were rendered useless to anything with a larger displacement than the sunken ferries now blocking the harbor entrance.

Basraistan's civil war did not end with the American departure. Approximately 30% of the remaining civilian population fled the country by the end of the year. The fighting dropped out of the headlines until the Summer of 2006 when Iran's revitalized armed forces (an accomplishment violating a dozen stern League of Nations resolutions) swept into Basraistan. Disorganized conflict gave way to systematic ethnic mass murder. An unofficial estimate could later only offer a guess at a toll of several tens of thousands. A similar fate befell the nation of Khuzestan—it was forcibly subsumed back into the national territory of Iran.

\* \* \* \* \*

The Global War had created vast number of refugees. They fled across national and natural boundaries to escape into camps which often had little more than rudimentary facilities. It is rarely mentioned in standard history books that 10 to 15 million people are estimated to have died in these camps and surrounding regions from a viral illness referred to as CAMP Fever, a mutated corona virus. The World Health Organization officially labelled it as Community-Acquired Malevolent Pneumonitis. Scant research was done on the affliction until it re-emerged in the Spring of 2007. A series of ecological disasters in South East Asia had created several large temporary cities along the Thailand-Burma-Laos border region. The disease is believed to have been re-ignited here, then spread south to Malaysia and west to the array of nations on the subcontinent. In the Autumn reports from Doctors Without Borders volunteers stated it was rapidly infecting refugees in Central and West Asia. By New Year's Day 2008 the first report of outbreaks in East Africa appeared; by late Spring, however, new cases in all three zones were no longer being found. The disease had disappeared except for those already infected. A mortality rate of 60% left hundreds of thousands dead. Treatment was often ineffective since the afflicted rarely were seen by a physician within the critical initial 48 hours.

Yet the First World took little note. A U.S. Presidential election with a glamorous name from the past commanded the obsession of all media formats—including the latest: interactive hologram bloggers.

# *Campaign 2008*

CORY STRATTON had been the epicenter of American politics until early December 1999. When his eldest son, Kenneth, was hospitalized as a result of sickle cell anemia, Stratton withdrew from the public spotlight. His son's subsequent death in March 2000 seemed also to end Stratton's public career.

Seven years later Stratton announced the creation of a foundation to administer a scholarship in his son's name. Stratton had maintained all the funds he received from the sale of his book ("An American Sojourn") in a special account. Investments in the burgeoning field of renewable energy had quadrupled the fund's assets. The leading product was being created at America's lunar base, Athena. Scientists and industrialists had combined their efforts to devise a panel that was highly absorbent of the solar radiation pouring onto Sentinella's surface. Their prospectus for investors said the panels would within a decade reduce the need for non-renewable energy sources by 50%. (The contamination of a financial service corporation's facility at Goose Pond, Connecticut on June 21, 2004, as a result of a significant accident at a nearby controversial power plant, compelled the research.)

Stratton was invited to discuss the foundation on the nation's pre-eminent afternoon all-media program, "Let's Talk!" with host Lottie Tailor. This program was viewable on multiple formats by an audience larger than any of the five major broadcast evening news presentations.

When she was a recent graduate of Tulane University, Ms. Tailor's reputation as an incisive interviewer began with her series of talks with Dr. Martin Luther King during his 1970 campaign for the U. S. Senate in Georgia. During the course of a week, as a correspondent for an Atlanta TV station, she was allowed to see most of the inner workings of the campaign. Day by day she brought Dr. King into homes across the State as a dedicated husband, father, minister and worker for the people. His chief issue was to make the provisions of the 1964 Civil Rights Act and the 1965 Voting Rights Act as the next Amendment to the Constitution. Although the Acts were established law each required periodic renewal by Congress.

Dr. King believed this could subject the provisions to manipulations at a later date; as part of the Constitution the provisions, and the rights of the people, would have strengthened safeguards.

[**Note:** Senator King's proposal was ratified as the 26th Amendment to the Constitution in 1982, during his second term in office.]

In the final interview of the series, Ms. Tailor drew Dr. King out of his reluctance to discuss Memphis 1968. In an unusually muted voice he related the events. "A march had been scheduled in the city to support a striking municipal workers' union. However, a thunderstorm and an early settlement of the strike changed my plans. The next day's headlines showed what might have been. In a boarding-house, nearby to a motel where I had reserved a room, I was told that one of the tenants had failed to properly close his room door. As another tenant exited her room across the hall, an open window allowed through a gust of wind. This pushed in her neighbor's door. On a chair in the room was a rifle.

I later heard that a telescopic sight was attached. The man was asleep on the bed. There were some beer cans on the floor. The woman ran to the manager, who called the police. The report of a gun brought them quicker than usual to the neighborhood. The man was arrested. I was told there was some evidence that implicated him and others in a plot..." (*Against you?*)...Yes. (*Do you think his being shot and killed at the courthouse by a sniper the following day was part of the conspiracy?*)...Only God knows for certain."

\* \* \* \* \*

Lottie Tailor won several TV and journalism awards as a result of the interviews, plus a program of her own.

Now sitting beside her was another person whose schedule had been changed by fate.

"General..."

"Ms. Tailor."

"Corrie."

"Lottie."

They laughed, and the studio audience joined in. Over the next uninterrupted hour and a half she encouraged him to relate the struggle he and his family confronted with Kenneth's illness, hospitalization and his final day. A man who had witnessed the demise of many in war, now with difficulty, discussed the death of one in a commentary at once clinical and deeply heart-breaking.

"And as a tribute, Corrie, you have Kenneth's Fund—the foundation created and named to honor your son."

"Yes...it's a means for my family and I to still have, in a way, a physical connection to Kenneth...Life each day is a remembrance of who went before. We set ourselves to follow their achievements, to avoid their mistakes. When we remember a loved one we conflict ourselves with memories of joy and sorrow. My family and I are blessed for having had Kenneth with us...for...a short time...we...strive to see the joy, the accomplishments rather than the sorrow. It's what any family strives to do with its memories. The foundation will help individuals and families strive to achieve what can be a better future for themselves and this nation."

"And you may yet strive to help the country in other ways?"

"Is that a question or a prediction?"

"Let's talk again in six months," concluded Lottie Tailor with a bemused smile.

\* \* \* \* \*

Since 1952 the number of States conducting a Presidential Preference Primary had grown every four years; by 2000 the States seemed on the verge of open hostilities in the jostling to be The First In The Nation primary. New Hampshire's demand to retain this status in Presidential election years was based on its assertion of a superior record in picking winners out of the pack. Political scientists dismissed the claim, pointing out that New Mexico was the true champion in the art of siding with future, or renewing, tenants at Washington's most distinguished public housing address. Since entering the Union in 1912 the "Land of Enchantment" had voted with the popular vote victor in every November Presidential election except in 1976.

Seeking to establish order to the process, the National Committees of the two major parties had agreed in 2006 on a revised format for the next round of primaries. A series of four regionally-based contests would be held on the third Tuesday of each month from March through June. The regions were set as the Northeast, the South, the Central Midwest and the West. Each would have a turn at being first over the years, but the initial first would be the Northeast. By great historical fortune Cory Stratton was a resident of New York. The State's Governor, Nelson Balboa, was determined to draft Stratton as a Favorite Son candidate in the Federalist Party primary. Unless Stratton was planning on physically restraining him boasted Governor Balboa, he would campaign non-stop for Stratton throughout all eleven States in the region. So, in a great pincer movement with his non-campaign Foundation activities and the Governor's unofficial draft movement, Cory Stratton rolled over his competition and forced them to smile about it. Stratton projected himself as he honestly was—straight forward, intelligent, committed to the All-American virtues of hard work, family and morality based on the loving-God teachings of a faith that had endured for centuries. He was no goody-goody fool; when aggravated by obstruction caused by arrogant, narrow-mindedness Stratton could unleash a verbal fury that few with combat experience cared to endure. Of course, this only helped to generate support for him. The common response by the public was, "Hey, if it bugs Stratton, who's as cool as ice, it must really be bad. Tell Cory to let the thunder roll." This last remark comes from a Persian Gulf War story concerning arguments Stratton had with the White House. He purportedly said, "We've hit them with the lightning (the month-long air and missile assault on Iranian targets), now we must let the thunder roll." (Unleashing an unrestricted armor-supported ground assault—with its goal being downtown Tehran).

Sensing they were in a no-win scenario Stratton's competition conceded him the Northeast, and redeployed their forces to the remaining regions. On Primary Day Eve, Cory Stratton finally made it official; he announced his candidacy on the steps of City Hall in Brooklyn, New York. He spoke to the nation, and gave fair warning to Edward Galway (the presumptive Libertarian candidate) that the political thunder was set to roll, with its goal being downtown Washington.

[In this history Brooklyn is a separate city from New York City, which has three boroughs.]

"We gather here today as Nature brings rebirth to our beloved land. This nation has also endured the long, dark bitterness of the passing political season. It is time now to go to work. We have much to do. What is vital and dynamic about our country has lain too long beneath the chilling by-product of a harsh era. An era when conflicts abroad created divisions at home. An era when politicians put moral words in their speeches, but not moral deeds in their actions. We have it within ourselves the ability to rise up this land, our nation, ourselves, to the sun-washed glory we have known. We can renew the luster of this great constellation of towns and cities, of rural and urban communities, and become again a gleaming beacon for the world to admire."

"We will be as a storm upon the prairie that sweeps away the Arctic chains, and restores robustness to the great heartland. We will let the thunder roll from coast to coast, from North to South, as a clarion call for renewal. We are better than what we have been! We can be as great as we once were!"

"Now is the hour to begin. I will do all I can to help you, this State, this region, this nation! I will seek the nomination for President, and I ask for the help of a few good citizens in this endeavor!"

"And so we begin again! God bless you and your family! God bless the United States of America!"

\* \* \* \* \*

Stratton secured a runaway victory, receiving 70% of the popular vote. The one surprise of the day was the 20% won by the little-known, second-term Governor of Ohio, Bertford (Bert) Maurus. He carried out a populist-style whirlwind campaign that bypassed the large cities to concentrate on the region's hinterland. It was here, Governor Maurus said, the strength of the nation resided. He called these people America's Indispensable Majority (A.I.M.), and he used "AIM" as the theme of his speeches.

"This country was not established by tycoons who bought land tracts and turned them into corporate parks and condo villages. America was built by workers, out there every day, doing it one plank of wood, one brick, one electric cable, one pipeline at a time. We use to have a grand concept for this nation. It helped us AIM higher, to AIM for the stars, to AIM for a society stretching from one great ocean to another. The countries at our borders are crumbling. If we don't take the right steps their weaknesses could cause us trouble. We must AIM to complete our Manifest Destiny, and establish the virtues and rewards of American Civilization for those now slipping backwards. We can AIM higher! Destiny will ensure our AIM!"

Governor Maurus' remarks alluded to the social turmoil brewing in Canada and Mexico. The Province of Quebec was scheduled to hold another plebiscite on independence two weeks after the 2008 U.S. Presidential election. The last such referendum, on October 30, 1995, was defeated by a margin of 1.2%; there were now indications that the result could go just as narrowly for the separatists. Some observers in Ottawa had long believed this campaign was really directed at securing a stronger voice for La Belle Province within the Canadian Confederation. "Independence" would be a bargaining chip in a new round of consultations with the other Provinces. Since 1995 something had changed in the rest of Canada. A pioneer-cowboy spirit existed in the minds and souls of many of those living west of Ontario; and, over the past several years that spirit had become a bit more cantankerous. The feeling was "If Quebec wants to go, let them go!" Westerners had come to the conclusion that nothing would satisfy the French-speakers, not even resettling them in France. In a small but influential circle Quebec's idea of separation gave rise to a similar concept for the West. Nationalism for Canadians had always been a rather nebulous concept. They were forced into a nation-state status in 1864 because of the growing concerns regarding the chaos to their south, which had been enflamed by the seizure of the Washington government by the Radical Unionists during the States War.

The Westerners were willing to say publicly what they considered obvious—what is Canada anyway, eh? The

Atlantic Provinces are an economic basket case. The Inuit had taken control of the Northern Territory. So where does that leave the West? Paying the bill for all the others? No way, no more!

Committees of political and business leaders began meeting in Alberta, British Columbia, Manitoba and Saskatchewan in early 2007 to vaguely probe their options. As the year progressed these Provincial committees established a regional working-group to co-ordinate their investigations. No one spoke openly on this development, other than to express concern regarding the uncertainty of the future. The mountain was privately considering coming to Mohammed. After a conference in late April 2008 a telephone call was placed to the Governor's office in Columbus, Ohio. An offer was made pertaining to a trade mission. It was agreed that Governor Maurus' top aide, Alex Poller, would travel to Vancouver the following week.

Alex Poller was a decorated hero of the Persian Gulf conflict, where he served as a Colonel in the U.S. Army Rangers. Poller's career was placed in jeopardy when he insisted upon repeating his criticisms of the Prescott Administration's policy of restraint in dealing with a vanquished Iran. On more than one occasion, in private discussions, Poller had come close to accusing then President Prescott of idiocy for failing to fully dismember Iran. A superior officer advised Poller that in his own best interest he should pursue his career goals elsewhere. Certain political elements at home were only too happy to latch onto a genuine looks-great-in-a-uniform hero as a means of attracting the media spotlight.

This faction with all its noise about a new approach to international policies, and what the military should be permitted to do, and how Congress could be a millstone for true patriots seeking to implement strategies which every knowledgeable American was certain to realize made unqualified sense, was actually a throwback to an earlier political generation. They saw foreign policy directives as the means of keeping foreigners away from America. Aid programs should be designed primarily to assist other nations in purchasing American-made weapons so that their own military could stand up to whatever regional bully confronted them. Economic policy would be designed to expand American exports to all nations regardless of any "messy" internal affairs review. These America-First true believers rationalized that a leading contributing factor to the demise of The People's Republics of Eurasia was its dependence on, perhaps addiction to, Western financing and cultural items. It was their firmly held conviction that the rope from which the West was to swing actually lassoed the East. "Just let us in the door," their business supporters clamored, "and we'll get them hooked. Then we'll buy and sell 'em like commodities."

This odd coalition of free marketers and neo-isolationists wanted to construct a bulwark of immigration and economic restrictions to tightly control access to America; they wanted a defense capability three to four times greater than any possible combination of adversaries. The world should accept American directives to improve their receptiveness to American exports, but on no account should nations expect anything beyond a minimal toehold within U.S. markets.

Alex Poller brought to this movement a front man for a dream held by many of its members—crafting the United States of North America. If Europe can strive to accomplish a workable union, if Soviet China is emerging as the dominant entity in Asia (with Nippon and Australia as consenting cohorts), then why shouldn't America expand to its natural and rightful extent? This concept for a drive towards a renewal of manifest destiny had germinated from various writings of disaffected, agitated nationalists who believed the Federal Government stood in the way of America's success. This group felt that Washington bureaucrats were too timid to propel the U.S. to its rightful place as not merely the pre-eminent world power, but the dominating global colossus. They sought a public voice who would be capable of eclipsing their media-generated image of a gun-totting fringe element. A ray of hope had dawned for them in the emergence of Alex Poller. This decorated veteran had sought a nomination for a House of Representatives seat in the 2000 election. However, the district he targeted was the home of a ten-year incumbent who said she would not disappear because some lobbyist group's shining knight arrived on the scene. Poller had to fight in a primary and he did it the only way he knew how—ambush and take no prisoners. Contributions flowed into Poller's campaign fund from a host of political action committees allied to the movement. Poller was well-armed and set for battle. In the military he rose through the ranks chiefly on his battlefield activities. Poller was always the first to volunteer for whatever action was at hand. Prior to the Persian Gulf War, Poller had seen action during the liberation of Cuba (1961), in the Philippines War (1972–84) and in the Central American conflicts (1983–90). He knew how to react in operations conceived and designed by others. Planning was not Poller's forte, yet he insisted on total control of the primary campaign. It was rough-edged and off-stride from the start and went downhill from there. Poller's reaction was to become more strident. In the single debate between the two candidates Alex Poller responded to the opening question ("Why should the voters consider selecting you?") by launching into a tirade against the very institution he sought to join. He denounced Congress as a cesspool of ineptness, corruption and as a nest of sycophants to foreign interests. At the depths of his diatribe Poller declared "the so-called leadership of Congress is not worthy of my respect. I would feel obligated to lie to them if it would advance a cause I championed."

What followed was not an intentional minute of silence; it simply took Poller's opponent, the moderator and the audience that long to recover from Poller's outburst. The moderator attempted to give him a chance to clarify his remarks, but Poller essentially ordered him to move on. With only a week left before the voting took place, Alex Poller did not have time to recover. For that matter, he did not see that he had any need to alter his remarks. His goal was not to revise the status quo but to upend it. He finished a very distant second. The incumbent was re-nominated with 85% of the vote. Defeat only convinced Poller of the need to adjust his tactics not his objectives.

Poller's fire and brimstone polemics drew the attention of a politician whose shallowness could make him acceptable to a public attuned to style rather than substance. Bert Maurus dreamed of being an up and coming power within the party; but, he not was passionately consumed by any issue. He could discern the general anxiety in the electorate and respond with plausible platitudes. Well and good, temporarily, for the Legion Hall dinner circuit, but political dynamics required something actually dynamic. Maurus admired Alex Poller's ability to stir, engage and occasionally nearly incite a crowd by the vehemence of his oratory. Nevertheless, Maurus was keenly aware of Poller's shortcomings. He could get the parade marching but left on his own the procession could have a lemmings-like outcome. Following his re-election as Governor in 2004, Maurus contacted Poller and offered him an advisory role on his staff. Poller gratefully accepted the post especially since the alternative was a future financed solely by his Army pension. The Governor's intention was to have Poller tarry on the fringes of his Administration to be available at the Governor's beckoning when a fiery tidbit was required. Alex Poller had an alternative agenda in mind; in less than three years he was Chief of Staff to a Presidential candidate.

Therefore, it came to pass that Alex Poller arrived at a conference of exacerbated leaders who were primed to hear the musings of a man ingrained with the belief that you cut to the heart of the matter best by using a bayonet. Poller met with the Premiers of Canada's four western Provinces at a hotel in Vancouver. Poller's own staff included a number of security assistants, who dutifully checked the conference suite for susceptibility to on or off-site surveillance. Poller had a definite opinion on what he would say to the four men, and wanted to be assured that no one else was aware of his remarks.

Poller spoke for the better part of an hour recounting much of what his listeners had themselves stated about Quebec. He outlined the future of a society where the number of those capable of contributing to the overall good would diminish (attributed to Quebec's departure and the Inuit's embargo on releasing resources from their territory without a premium payment in other than Canadian dollars). All of this would place an increasing burden on the prosperous western Provinces to provide for the less developed Atlantic region.

One Premier acted as a devil's advocate and challenged Poller to explain why they would not be accused of Quebec-style separatism and disloyalty to the Confederation. Poller responded with an assertion that any contract, whether between individuals or political entities, is only binding as long as all parties adhere to the provisions. Quebec's abandonment of its responsibilities under the nation-building accord rendered the entire system dysfunctional. The western Provinces would not be abrogating their commitments as their obligations would be negated by Quebec's precipitous actions. It would then fall to the western Premiers to chart their future in the most advantageous way possible. Naturally, since they share a good working relationship the four could envision a compact regional affiliation. However, in an ever increasingly complex and competitive global marketplace such a downsized unit might find itself at a distinct disadvantage. Perhaps in reviewing their options the Premiers might entertain other arrangements.

Again, the devil's advocate spoke out. What if the electorate in Quebec again rejected independence? What if the separatists had gone to the well once too often? What if we are left with another narrow margin scenario and with Quebec still loudly dissatisfied with its place in the Confederation?

Alex Poller looked each of the men in the eye and sternly advised them. "If I were you I would do all that I could to ensure an outcome that would allow for a future action that would be in the best long-term interest of my constituency. If someone else required assistance in facilitating a course of action which would enhance my own options, I would provide appropriate accommodations to their needs."

For a final time the devil's advocate spoke. He alluded to the U.S. political situation. The primary season was nearly complete, and the candidate of Poller's choice while still in the running was not the odds-on favorite. Poller replied, "You have your work to do, I have mine." They agreed to talk again, conditional upon the outcome of their short-term endeavors.

# The Western Showdown

THE NOMINATION PROCESS had come to resemble two contending forces stalking one another, engaging in tactical strikes while maueuvering for a climatic encounter. The campaign for the selection of the Federalist Party Presidential candidate had developed into a head-to-head struggle between Cory Stratton and Bert Maurus. Stratton had achieved a narrow victory in the second round (The Southern region). Texas Senator A.B.E. Connell had sought a boost from his home territory, but he decided to withdraw when Texas was his lone triumph on voting day.

What was obvious, and yet unspoken, about the contest came to the forefront during the Southern phase. Cory Stratton was the first Black (male or female) to be considered a serious candidate for President in either major party. In the initial clamor the issue of racial background was not a prime topic. Yet because the South would vote following the opening hoopla, this would allow the public's natural bluntness to draw attention to the subject.

The history of racial discrimination and animosity in the United States reached back to colonial era policy of Britain engaging in the abduction of people in Africa and then subjecting these individuals to the horrors of slavery. This abomination transported tens of thousands of children, women and men to the American colonies and spawned a social tragedy that still afflicts the land of the free.

Cory Stratton was asked by a reporter how he felt about being the first Black likely to be elected President. Stratton responded, "I am, of course, proud of my African-Caribbean heritage. But I am not seeking the Presidency to represent just one ethnic group. A President must be mindful of the views and needs of everyone in America. I am keenly aware of the emotional and symbolic significance many people associate with my efforts. If what I do contributes to a better understanding between all the people of this country then I will have been successful, regardless of any personal political outcome. America is a unique concept. People come here from all over the world now by choice. They want to contribute to a society based on the inalienable rights proclaimed in our Declaration of Independence. I seek to be President because I want to defend these rights, and extend them to anyone who is today deprived of such rights because of injustice or intolerance."

In a region some expected to be hostile to Stratton, he found instead warm support from all racial groups. The one event that caused the Secret Service to tighten the security around Stratton occurred on Primary Day while he was in Chicago.

# The Lincoln Hotel Incident

May 20, 2008

THE WORK FOR THE Central-Mid West Primaries was now up to the labor-intensive, get-out-the-vote function of the local organizations. Cory Stratton had no rallies scheduled for the morning or afternoon. Still he was up and ready to go by 5:30 AM. The events described here were not reported at the time by either the local or national media at the direct request of the Secret Service. Although the Presidential candidates did not have a detail of Secret Service Agents assigned to them, the agency kept track of security anomalies. Following this day's incident outside The Lincoln Hotel in Chicago all the Presidential candidates were assigned a team of agents.

A tragedy was averted because a dog sat down. Chicago Police Officer Tracey Richards was out for an early morning jog before reporting for duty. She was part of the security operation at O'Hare Airport. Along for the run was her "partner," Max, from the K-9 unit. Most days Officer Richards and Max (a specially trained Labrador) ran along the Lake shoreline. Today she had decided on a city street course. At 6:17 she turned a corner and approached the vicinity of The Lincoln Hotel, which was across the street from her position. She could see the detail of CPD officers standing outside the building. One of them recognized her and waved. She waved back as she proceeded along. A delivery van was parked on her side of the four-lane boulevard across from the hotel's main entrance. The driver appeared to be checking a list. Officer Richards was about three paces past the driver's door when she noticed that Max was no longer at her side. He ran without a leash, a small technical impropriety.

She made a slight turn and froze. Max was sitting down and facing towards the driver. Officer Richards quickly drew her badge and service handgun from beneath her sweatshirt. She retraced her steps and was now in front of the van. In a voice loud enough to be heard across the then fortunately lightly travelled street she yelled out, "Chicago Police! Driver, get out of the van!"

The driver hesitated. Two officers from the hotel detail sprinted towards the van, guns drawn.

Officer Richards yelled again, "Chicago Police! Get out of the van!"

The driver seemed to move, and then slumped forwards. Officer Richards pulled open the door near her, as the other door was opened by one of her colleagues. The driver was foaming from the mouth. She checked his pulse, fading, nearly stopped.

"Call 911! We need an ambulance!" she shouted to the other officers.

The third officer now opened the side cargo door. "Damn! We need the bomb squad first!"

When the van's contents were examined it revealed enough of a nitrate-fuel mix to kill or severely maim anyone within 100 yards. The driver had killed himself with a cyanide tablet. Despite an exhaustive search by the Secret Service and the FBI the driver's identity could not be established. The van and the contents could not be traced.

There was no direct evidence of an assassination plot against Cory Stratton, but the Secret Service's view was "Believe that it is until proven otherwise."

The Chicago Police released a statement that the response to scene of a large number of emergency service personnel was due to a leaky propane tank in the van. The driver had apparently died of a heart attack before he could call for help.

Max was trained as an explosives locator. When he caught a certain scent he was to sit down facing the object.

The Stratton campaign moved on with an added sense of alertness. Stratton's top staff members talked among themselves about President Rockefeller's close call in Dallas 45 years earlier.

\* \* \* \* \*

The campaign in the Central-Mid West had been clarified when Representative Lori Ann Nasus announced that she was ending her quest for the nomination. She had decided to accept a standing offer to be a political consultant for World Network News. Her final press release included the statement "campaigning is no longer about discussing the issues. It is simply a commercial that's gotten way out of hand."

The region was Governor Maurus' home base. He had good rapport with the party's organization in the neighboring States. Along with the support of traditional line leadership here, which dated its philosophy to the inward-directed policies of a powerful Senator of 50 years earlier, Governor Maurus was able to do well enough to achieve a virtual tie with Cory Stratton in the number of committed delegates to the July Convention. June became the decisive month in the contest, as the candidates headed for California (with the largest delegation) and its satellite members of the Western region.

Economic refugees had long been a tough reality facing the four American States along the 1951-mile border with Mexico. The autocratic Popular Revolutionary Movement (MPR) was seeking to regain its stranglehold on power after narrowly losing the Presidency in the prior election. Shock waves of disorder had jolted the country over the past 6 years; more than once was suspicion aroused concerning the directing force behind the violence. Active, armed revolts were occurring in southern Mexico, and the Durango drug cartel was steadily corrupting an ever-growing number of government and military officers. In the prior election campaign the two political groups in opposition to the MPR had formed an alliance, nominated the same candidate, and aided by a virtual army of international observers had secured a victory by an extremely narrow margin. The incumbent was barred by Mexico's Constitution from running for a second term. For the upcoming Presidential election the alliance held together and again nominated a joint candidate. The MPR still controlled many key State Governorships, and this group was broadly hinting they would not acknowledge any result overseen by foreigners. The MPR Governors claimed the press and League of Nations observers were fronting for subversive elements.

All of this propelled thousands of improvised Mexicans to make the often hazardous journey to communities north of the border. Many were caught and sent back; nevertheless, a steady flood of desperate people seeking a better life ran, swam or crawled through whatever gap they could find in the Corrugated Curtain (the network of steel barriers along the border). Mexico could not provide for these people—its own citizens- and the Western Border States did not want to provide for them, yet on they came.

Bert Maurus brought to this emotional tinderbox a message of stark, dispassionate social myopia. There must be no consideration of any remedy other than to close the Curtain and keep it closed. Anyone in the U.S. illegally must be returned to their country of origin—whether or not that country wanted them. Maurus clothed such opinions in velvet rhetoric. He would speak first of the hard-working American-born laborers, of their economic plight, of their struggle to claim some of the star dust of the American Dream. Maurus acknowledged the difficulties of the refugees, while pleading for a "practical" analysis of the issue. Maurus' basic argument was "If America must be care-giver to the world, if we must accept all the misfortunate, untrained, uneducated souls of the earth, and struggle for years attempting to raise them up to the standards enjoyed by responsible, industrious Americans—we will bankrupt ourselves."

Cory Stratton had known arduous tasks from his career in the Marines. Parris Island almost became a fond memory compared to the incessant frenzy of the Western campaign. It was a life of virtual reality conducted within the realm of television, radio and web-broadcast studios. Stratton's favorite aspect of politics was the one-to-one meetings with voters. He could ask direct questions of actual folks and receive answers not processed analysis from researchers. The vastness of the region (from the Pacific coast to the Great Plains equalled nearly a third of the national territory), and the importance of every delegate, required a candidate's presence simultaneously at various sites. Television was regretfully the most efficient means of achieving the objective. Web broadcasts might have the potential to reach a larger audience, but the denizens of Web World had less of an interest in public policy than most other social groups.

Stratton's desire to express his ambitions for the future, his hopes for an emphasis on an individual's responsibility for the course of their own life became lost in restraints imposed by interviewer's scripts. The various chat shows, superficially designed as local soft-news oriented programs, were enthusiastic about offering Stratton a platform. It would surely give their station a boost in the ratings. "Yes, indeed, electing a President is a commendable civic undertaking. Certainly, it was thrilling to have such a dynamic personality on the show highlighting the major topics all citizens should turn their attention to at the proper time. Mr. Stratton...Cory, if I may... could you wrap it up into a few good sound bites. After all, shouldn't five and a half minutes be enough?"

The televised debates did not provide any more fruitful opportunity for expansive discourse. Stratton had suggested earlier in the year abandoning the standard format of replying to questions posed by a moderator, without being able to speak directly to an opponent. He preferred to face Governor Maurus without such a filter; and, he requested that they meet on a stage, sit at a table and question and reply in a normal conversation. Maurus would not consider it and accused Stratton of wanting to back out of the debates. Reluctantly, Stratton accepted what he could not alter; but, he devoted his closing remarks in the first debate to a challenge for a direct face-off and the abandonment of an outmoded format which politicians used to give mini-speeches rather than reply to specific inquiries.

The ballot counting should have been the easiest part of the Western campaign. California led the nation in the use of computerized voting machines. Unfortunately, it also led the nation in delays caused by voters who mangled their turn at the machines. It was not until the afternoon of the second day following the election that Cory Stratton was declared the very narrow victor. Delegates were elected from zones based on a State's Congressional districts. Stratton won in northern California, Oregon, Washington State, Idaho, Montana, the Dakotas and Utah. Maurus picked up delegates in southern California, Nevada, New Mexico, Arizona, Colorado and Wyoming. The final overall delegate count gave the nomination to Stratton by 70 votes from a total of 2509.

Strategists within the party besieged Stratton with calls for a statesman-like decision which would greatly aid party unity and the Fall campaign. Stratton's initial response was "HELL NO!" He threatened to court-martial (meaning "fire") anyone on his staff who spoke in favor of the proposal. A change in his viewpoint began to surface when Stratton was confronted with media speculation concerning a party-rending split over wording in the Convention's policy declaration. Unofficial sources claimed that Maurus was considering mounting an attempt to gain control of the

Platform Committee, which would write the declaration. Stratton was advised he had one chance to avoid such a disastrous spectacle. He must offer Governor Maurus the Vice Presidential nomination.

Stratton, against his better judgement, agreed to invite the Governor to his suite at the St. Francis Hotel in San Francisco, which had been his headquarters for the Western campaign. They met on the Saturday following the vote.

Bertford Edison Maurus, a middle-aged, middle-sized product of Middle America. He was once described by a commentator as a classic example of a harried, high school principal. Maurus' most notable characteristic was his earnest ability at promoting himself. Throughout his school years Maurus was well-known by other students; although when those classmates were interviewed in later years they often had difficulty recalling why they had liked Maurus at the time. One of his political opponents dubbed Maurus the "Cotton Candy Man." "He makes you want to have him, but afterwards you're left with a vague recollection of nothingness." Maurus was the quintessential organization man who got along by going along. He looked reasonably good in photographs, and was reasonably pleasant in person. No one in the party considered him an obstacle to their own potential, so no one put roadblocks in his path. Early on Maurus made himself available to the party leadership as a sacrificial candidate against entrenched incumbents. Maurus bided his time, racking up points he later converted into a legitimate nomination. He steadily worked his way up from County Commissioner to the State Assembly and the State Senate. Maurus' advancement to the Governor's Mansion was aided by a brawling primary battle that left the other party's organization in tatters.

"Why make an attempt at the Presidency from a base of obscurity?" a reporter bluntly inquired when Maurus announced his candidacy. "Who but a poli-sci nerd knew much about Milton Prescott or Jeff De Witt before they crawled out of the woodwork?" Maurus retorted. To himself he added, "The American system of government is open to those crafty enough to grab the public's attention just long enough to get a desired outcome."

The major fault in this concept was that Maurus had nothing to grab said attention...until. When perennial independent Presidential candidate Ray Oberauer re-emerged on the scene in 2004 he unleashed shrill rhetoric on the topic of foreign-born workers "stealing" American jobs. Maurus knew many people agreed with this view, but they were reluctant to openly endorse it with only an oddity such as Oberauer as the main proponent. When Maurus raised the topic with his aide Alex Poller he saw the other man's eyes light up with malevolent glee. "That's our ticket to Washington," chuckled Poller. "America has nothing to fear except a wretched refugee seeking to breed free-of-charge."

Thus, a campaign was born based on appealing to concerns about a volatile future populated increasingly by desperate people seeking escape from threats economic and lethal; and, a candidate came to meet the one obstacle remaining before his final objective.

"Governor Maurus, I'm glad you accepted my request to meet here. We have a better chance at privacy," said Cory Stratton as he met his visitor.

"I was delighted, General. It's an honor and a privilege for me to be in the presence of the next President of the United States."

"You're getting a bit ahead of events. Come in, there's a very good couch which I've made little use of. Is coffee OK? I don't have anything stronger on hand."

"Thanks, coffee will do fine. I should be able to hold out until cocktail hour."

They entered a sitting room with a dramatic view of the city. Stratton spoke briefly with an aide, who returned in a few minutes with a coffee pot, a pair of mugs, milk and sugar containers, and plates of fruit and Danish. After pouring the coffee the aide (a retired Marine Corps Sergeant who could pass for a 49ers offensive linesman) left the General and the Governor to continue their discussion.

Characteristically blunt Stratton looked Maurus in the eyes and declared, "Maurus, you're not my first or hundredth choice for Vice President. You take liberties with emotional issues and compound them with anxiety. My background is in solid teamwork. I cannot have, I will not tolerate, self-aggrandizing commandos running amuck and disrupting my strategy. If you sign on it means you park your ego somewhere safe. I will respect your opinions, I will consider your input, but you will abide by the final decision which I will make. "

"General," replied Governor Maurus, "Politics has been my professional career. Of course, I did my service for this great nation. Yep, two years in the State Militia Reserve."

[**Note:** In this history the SMR is a non-combat unit that is primarily a pool of office workers that assists the National Guard.]

Maurus paused, anticipating some comradely military chatter from Stratton; what he received was a stony, cold glare. "As I was saying, politics has been the major force in my life. I understand the process. I know how to interpret the core belief behind someone's public posturing. In this endeavor I'm the hard-nose veteran. Your straightforward, novice enthusiasm is certainly refreshing. It attracts the attention of voters who have chosen to become cynical. They don't understand the process. Of course, they're always delighted when our labors result in projects directed at their home town—no special interest boondoggle then. Yet its heaven forbid if somewhere else gets a slice of the pie. To them it means we're not doing our job correctly. All that mealy-mouth whining about closed door deals."

"Most people don't comprehend national issues, or don't want to be bothered. Just give them what they need to succeed on a day-to-day basis and they're happy. A politician who wants to be a leader realizes he must be seen to have a response to topics which the media propels into the headlines. Quite often the only way we can grab the public's attention is by going over the top. If we perform like college professors and explain, explain everything it comes across as so much blah-blah-blah. The people tune us out."

"Politics is the last surviving act of vaudeville. It may seem as if we're no more than a travelling circus act, nevertheless this is how the job gets done. The military confronts hard reality. Therefore, it requires a different response mode. Government is about romancing the source—whether it's the source of a bureaucratic decision, a legislative vote or a personal contribution. You gotta learn to 'walk the walk, talk the talk.' I'll play by your rules General 'cause you're the main game in town. Just don't shut me out. I can help you survive behind enemy lines."

Stratton was silent for several minutes. "So you want the position," he said regretfully in a declarative question.

"It will be a great honor and..." Maurus began. He cut himself short when Stratton abruptly snorted. "Yes, sir. I do accept your offer," he concluded quickly.

They stood and stiffly shook hands. Perhaps beckoned by an unseen signal Stratton's aide was at the door.

"The Sergeant will escort you to the elevator, Governor."

"Thank you again, General. I'm looking forward to the Convention."

Once they departed Stratton went to the washroom and scrubbed his hands.

# In Convention Assembled

NEW YORK STATE'S GOVERNOR, Nelson Balboa, was having a very busy, very productive year. He had been one of the leading advocates for Cory Stratton's entrance into the campaign for the nomination. On a second front, Balboa worked overtime to complete a task begun the previous year. The party's National Committee had agreed to hold the quadrennial nominating fete in his State. Moreover, for his unique candidate Balboa acquired a unique venue—the recently refurbished Ebbets Field, the home of Major League Baseball's Atlantic Division's pre-eminent franchise: the Brooklyn Dodgers. The Field had been initially renovated 50 years earlier, with assistance from the City of Brooklyn's taxpayers as the price for retaining the team. In 1957 the incumbent Mayor of New York City opposed a similar plan for the Polo Grounds, home of the baseball N.Y. Giants. The decision cost the region a team, and the Mayor his renomination.

In 1958 Ebbets Field became the first professional sports facility in the country to be encased in a dome. This game of the Boys of Summer was never intended to be played in the frost and icy rains of the Northeast's early Spring. The re-born ballyard could now accommodate 60,000 fans, and offered exquisite luxury for corporate sponsors in a ring of sky boxes. The dome was redesigned in the early 21st Century make-over to be retractable. This allowed sunlight to flow once more on the natural grass in the outfield; and on Autumn afternoons when the top was down the Yogi-ism that "it gets late early out there" once again applied.

At the completion of the baseball season, the Field becomes the playing ground for the region's junior National Football League member: the Titans. Baseball's nearly perennial champion, the N.Y. Yankees (of the Northern Division), and the NFL N.Y. Giants shared the historic grounds of Yankee Stadium.

[**Note:** In this history Major League Baseball is a single league with six divisions.]

Governor Balboa had made his request to MLB as soon as he learned that the team would be on an extended road trip in the first half of July. This would give the National Committee enough time to transform the Field into a convention site. A platform floor would be overlaid above the grass and dirt surfaces to spare it from the trampling by an expected crowd of over 55,000 people (comprised of delegates, alternate delegates, their families, special guests, the news media and security personnel.)

Opening Day, as everyone fell into the habit of calling it, was Monday July 7th. Long gone was the era when political conventions could drone on for the better (worse?) part of a week. The parties knew the event must be packaged as a prime-time special. They would have two days to showcase their best and brightest. Deadlocked conventions with multiple ballots had become extinct in the age of hyped-up primary election results.

Cory Stratton would not make an appearance in public or at the Field until the time of his acceptance speech, scheduled for 9 PM Eastern Time Tuesday evening. Until then it was the delegates' picnic. Many arrived a week early and spent their time gawking in the usual manner of tourists. A great number of delegates and their families arrived by train; they wanted to be enthralled by the classical and austere Pennsylvania Railroad Station in Manhattan, which was even now preparing for 2010 and the 100th anniversary of its opening.

[In 1963 Jacqueline Kennedy, the spouse of then former Vice President John Kennedy who was later elected to two terms as President, led an effort that saved the Romanesque architectural splendor of Penn Station from demolition. Her support also aided the passage of landmark preservation laws in the Tri-City region of Brooklyn, New York and Newark.]

The delegates were headquartered along Hotel Row, which was built above Manhattan's Second Avenue subway line. The transit authority provided a special series of trains to run from the hotels to Ebbets Field's subway stop of Flatbush Avenue during the two-week period. The Stratton entourage was settled into the Presidential Suite at downtown Brooklyn's appropriately four-starred Marriott Hotel.

Among the attractions to visit in the region were:

—Wally Datbow's entertainment complex of film, play and stage show theaters standing along Manhattan's First Avenue between 42nd and 48th Streets.

—The Long Acre Reservoir which encompassed the former Times Square district. Redevelopment plans for this previously most seedy of Manhattan neighborhoods had been launched thirty years earlier. Buildings were levelled or moved, huge new foundation pits were excavated, and then it all slammed to a halt because of relentless litigation unleashed by developers competing for contracts in the project. After a quarter century of court battles, and a Federal inducement of considerable tax credits, the combatants surrendered the land to the City's Environmental Protection

Agency. A small lake and park were eventually established on the site, which had previously been named for a newspaper once housed there. The publication had folded in 1962 as the victim of a protracted contract dispute between management and labor.

—For outdoor enthusiasts the unspoiled nature reserve of the Meadowlands was just across the Hudson River.

# Tuesday, July 8th

SHORTLY BEFORE SUNRISE a high-level wind over the Tri-City metropolitan area began to stir, delivering cooler air from the West. For several days prior a thermal inversion had parked above the region trapping pollution and waste heat in an already sultry air mass. The dawn's early light reflected in dazzling luminance from many of the high-rise structures, including the landmark Home Office Building of the Pinnacle Insurance Company near Madison Square Park. With the change in the weather the delegates felt free to express their enthusiasm for what The Brooklyn Eagle newspaper proclaimed as "Stratton's Surging Sojourn."

This would be the first Convention to reflect recent changes in the Union—the addition of Puerto Rico as the 51st State, and the transfer of the residential portions of the City of Washington, D.C. to the jurisdiction of the State of Maryland—which at last provided them with full representation in Congress.

Ebbets Field was almost literally packed to the rafters as the session was called to order at 1 PM. This would allow for speeches officially placing Cory Stratton and Bert Maurus before the Convention as candidates. No ambitious office-holder, no potential office-seeker wanted to be denied their 15 minutes of fame in declaring their loyalty to the nominees.

At 8 PM "America The Beautiful," the National Anthem, was played to initiate the evening session; as the final phrase of the first verse "...from sea to shining sea." was sung by the crowd, Governor Balboa rose to begin the ubiquitous "Man Who" speech. This would be followed by the acclamatory votes of endorsement, and what the organizers advertised as a stirring biographical film on Stratton. All would be ready for the 9 PM grand moment in time.

As the last of the cheers re-echoed off the domed ceiling, as the final credits of the film rolled past on the four very large screens set around the Field, the lights stayed dimmed. Slowly, section by section the vast throng fell silent, in questioning anticipation of what seemed a delay in the scripted proceedings. The pause had been calculated. The thunder was about to roll, and this was the lull before the storm.

Tentatively a soft, lilting note wafted through the enclosure. Off-stage in a runway leading to the playing area a musical instrument was being put to use. Its tonal production was steadily increased, and now all could clearly hear. The solitary instrumental voice did more to hold those gathered in captive rapture than any throaty roar. Then, from the opposite side of the Field a companion instrument answered; then a third, then a score. The lights now spotlighted the instrument players as they proceeded towards the podium.

In total 108 bagpipe players (two for each delegation—the territories of Guam, Samoa and the Virgin Islands were also represented) marched in the stylized cadence of the song they performed. "Amazing Grace" resonated throughout the building. Everyone not already on their feet was now standing, jumping, shouting and at least attempting to sing the lyrics. Cacophonous was too polite a description for the auditory mayhem that erupted within Ebbets Field. Spotlights that had been bathing the euphoric throng in alternating tides of red, white and blue brought an abrupt cessation to the raucous outpouring when the beams were dramatically focused at once upon the speaker's podium. Shouted commands went from floor mangers for the delegates to be silent. As a wave retreats from a shoreline the noise dissipated—momentarily.

A military bugle let loose a single note and a figure emerged from the shadows to stand in the center of the floodlit stage. He waved to the crowd. Instant recognition produced instant pandemonium. Cory Stratton, attired in a classical business executive's dark suit, with white dress shirt and dashing red silk tie, raised his arms and then saluted the Convention. Cheers, shouts and blasts from air horns and plastic tooters roared backed the delegates' reply. The de riguer well-rehearsed "spontaneous" parade of delegations swept across the floor. The New York State delegates, situated front and center before the podium, were doing their Empire State best to out-shout everyone else.

Stratton could do no more than wave and laugh. He walked along the edge of the stage acknowledging individuals known to him by pointing and giving a thumbs-up signal. The demonstrations seemed capable of going on all night; actually the floor managers were timing the event. It would be allowed to run for ten minutes, and then curtailed. A national television, radio and Internet audience was waiting for the true business of the evening.

Stratton was given a cue. He stepped to the microphone and began calling out "Thank you, thank you...thank you, delegates!" Exhaustion, as much as the barked orders from the managers, soon quieted the crowd. The light beyond the podium faded. Cory Stratton stood out from the Field's shadows in a golden circle of light.

"Thank you! I haven't seen or heard such excitement since my barracks at Parris Island got its first week-end pass!"

*(Shouts of "Semper Fi!" rang from the Field.)*

"I am humbled by the great honor you have bestowed

upon me this evening. I am glad my family can be here with me...I wish there was one other..."

He stopped, unable to continue. A silence so deep it seemed impossible in such a setting swept through the arena. They all knew to whom he was referring.

From the twilight of a corner a solitary figure emerged, and proceeded to where Cory Stratton stood. It was Elizabeth, his spouse. They embraced and kissed.

This display ignited the crowd. Everyone jumped to their feet again, cheering again, applauding again, crying softly or loudly.

The Stratton's children joined them at center stage. Joyful pandemonium engulfed the floor of the Convention. Delegates were chanting "Strat—tons! Strat-tons!" over and over. Five minutes went by, and still it all continued. Only exhaustion curtailed the demonstration after nearly eight minutes.

The Stratton family stood in a close circle, then turned and waved to the delegates. Mrs Stratton led the children back to their seats.

Once more Cory Stratton was a solitary figure in the spotlight of the Convention, of the news media and of history.

"Thank you."

Once more cheers erupted, for two minutes this time.

In a voice that was initially soft-spoken, but which grew in strength, he began. "I pledge to you I will dedicate all I do between now and November 4th to fulfill your hopes. We begin today a great sojourn..."

*(Cheers and applause.)*

"...to restore the integrity of the American people's Government!"

*(A flurry of hoop-la on the floor.)*

"The task ahead is not easy. It requires a deep commitment to duty. Many Americans are ashamed of the State of the Union. 'Politician' has become a foul word, rather than the title of an honorable servant of the people. A Government position has too often become the fast-track for acquiring questionable personal rewards from those seeking to do business with the nation. Officials in Washington now seem to spend more time dining with possible future employers than working for the people."

"Election campaigns have become fat-wallet, free-for-alls, with glossy, glib, distorted messages replacing well-reasoned presentations of alternative view points. The vast majority of Americans do not engage in such behavior, and they do not support it! We have been too long silent in our opposition. We must proclaim our demands for reform! It's time to let the thunder roll!"

*(Full-scale, full-throated enthusiasm throughout the Field.)*

"I have spent most of my adult life in service to this great nation of ours. My parents came to America seeking the freedom they were denied in their homeland."

*(A wave of applause swept across the crowd.)*

"They made America their new homeland. America is my home! And I want the world to again marvel at our society!"

*(Chants of "USA!" "USA!" "USA!" as red, white and blue lights washed over the gathering.)*

"The beneficial dynamics of liberty, justice and democracy are not exclusive to America. Nevertheless, the people of the world recognize America as the hallowed ground of these essential human rights. We can best guarantee freedom here at home by helping to safeguard freedom everywhere. Such a commitment requires a long term, fully dedicated response. We cannot transact a 'drive-by' liberation of a country facing an external or internal threat to its freedom. Planning only for the short-term leads to disasters like Basraistan."

"In my career experience I know that well-designed plans must always provide for the option to adjust to circumstances. We cannot make commitments and then expect events to follow according to plan. Reality changes planning. We must encourage other nations to carry out political, economic and social reforms. These steps will help strengthen and secure their societies. Rigid ideologies are a trap, leading only to a dead end. History changes dogma. How many empires and nations have declared themselves the fulfillment of history's intent, and then collapsed when the tide of history swept them away because they were unwilling to grow? We must always defend freedom and be willing to adjust our strategy to the nature of events on the ground."

*("Let the thunder roll!" "Let the thunder roll!")*

"The Albertson and Galway Administrations gave scant attention to our troubled world. Ignoring problems doesn't make them go away. This nation, this planet needs a Government in Washington that understands the consequences of events, even in far away countries of which we may know little about. My Administration..."

*(Shouts of "President Stratton!" "President Stratton!" boomed out from the crowd.)*

"...my Administration will be dedicated to protecting America's freedom by effectively assisting other nations in dealing with global-ramification issues. We do not need, and the people of the world cannot afford, further tragedies such as we have seen in Korea and West Asia."

*(Prolonged, respectful applause.)*

"It would be far too easy for me to say that I have already done enough for my country. Campaigning for office is as arduous for my family as it is for me. I spend very long periods of time away from them. My dear wife, Libby, did her best to talk me out of running. She knows that for any man the quest for the Presidency can be one of travail. For a black man the quest can be one of peril. We spend too much time dividing ourselves into categories, and manufacturing excuses about differences. Before God, before the Constitution, before the rest of the world, there are no differences among us—we are all Americans!"

*(The band ignites a boisterous rally by playing "This Is My Country!")*

"I have never been involved in politics before..."

*("Good for you!")*

"I frequently said to voters during the primaries 'I may need some time learning the game.' Their reply usually was 'It's better that you don't know the game. This way we can believe you when you say you're going to change it.'"

*("Let the thunder roll!" "Let the thunder roll!")*

"I reflected long and hard about the prospect of seeking the Presidency. I was awed by the possibilities, embarrassed by the expectations and nearly daunted by the obstacles. Couldn't I leave it to someone else? I am not a second George Washington. I am simply an ordinary citizen hoping to make America a better place for my family and friends, for others living here now and for future generations. I have no magic formula. Military strategies cannot resolve social, economic or ecological problems. As our nation's land defense forces are built up from the squad, our nation's society is built up from the family. My Administration..."

*(Cheers, applause and air horns.)*

"...will be dedicated to a return to basic training..."

*(Laughter and applause.)*

"...for this nation. If the family is secure with a good home, with a good job for either or both parents, with a good school for the children, with top-quality health care available to all, with everyone having an abiding respect for all others in the family, the community, the State, the Nation and the world—we begin again the soujourn to a better life for all this planet's children of God!"

*(Standing ovation and rapid-pace demonstrations.)*

"With humility to guide me, I asked myself if I let someone else do it, will I be satisfied if they only partially succeed? I will honestly pray that if President Galway..."

*(Mild booing.)*

"No! Stop that! You will respect the man and the office he holds!"

*(Silence. Then applause starts slowly, finally sweeping throughout the Field.)*

"I will honestly pray that if President Galway is re-elected that he will succeed in making America a better place for all."

*(Applause again.)*

"If someone else partially succeeds, or if misfortune befalls them and they fail, how would I judge myself? You, the American people, have seen something in my character which you appreciate. I have sat with some of you in your living rooms, in diners, at meeting halls and sometimes in your pick-up trucks, plainly talking about America's future. You wish to put a great responsibility on my shoulders. You believe I can step up to this challenge and succeed."

*("You bet you can! Cory Can Do It! Cory Can Do It!")*

"Whatever success I can achieve will not be merely a personal or partisan success. It will be an American success!"

*("Let the thunder roll!")*

"This great nation of ours is a constellation of villages, towns and cities woven together forming a glittering banner of hope for the entire world. To societies still in the grip of tyranny the Light of Liberty shinning in the majestic harbor of this remarkable metropolitan region is still an inspiration. We owe it to ourselves, we owe it to all the people of the world to keep the fire of freedom burning brightly!"

*(Cheer, applause and floor demonstrations led by New York State.)*

"How does any President…"

*("President Stratton!" President Stratton!")*

Now in a bolder, more determined cadence Stratton continued.

"How does any President deal with the array of compelling needs and conflicting interests of a country spanning a continent from sea to shining sea? It is not easy. For all the power of the Oval Office, a President soon realizes how limited that power is. Congress, State Governments, budget restraints and other political factors can, and do, limit a President's options.

And yet, 1600 Pennsylvania Avenue is a focal point of

enormous influence. A President is called upon to lead this nation, to provide a stellar moral and political example, to embody the guiding spirit of earlier, great Presidents. A President must balance reality, hope and dreams."

"Reality is the necessary acceptance of compromise. Hope is the vision which sees beyond the limitations of daily existence. Dreams, nutured in the warm textured sunlight of the imagination, are the seeds of a new and better reality."

"A successful President is one who is capable of using these concepts, and who can build upon the public's trust gathered through a lifetime of dedicated service to this great nation, and bring America to where she needs to be!"

"We can succeed! America can succeed!"

"We will let the thunder roll from coast to coast, from North to South, as a clarion call for renewal! We are better than what we have been! We can be as great as we once were!"

"Yes, I accept your nomination!"

"Let's get to work!"

"And so we begin again!"

"God bless you and your family!"

"God bless The United States Of America!"

\* \* \* \* \*

Into a sea of chanting, cheering, delirious delegates went the final words of Cory Stratton's acceptance speech. Into the air alive with the electricity of human emotions came cascading ballons, streamers and confetti. All the Field's lights went up on Stratton's conclusion. The noise rose and spiralled, echoing off the walls and the dome, a continuous wave with an almost physical impact.

Stratton, having stood alone at the podium, was now surrounded by his wife and children, his brothers and sisters, other relatives, plus various politicians. For an obligatory photo-op Stratton stood with upraised arms, shoulder to shoulder, with Bert Maurus. As soon as decently possible

Maurus was led to the side, officially to greet his home State delegation that was positioned near the podium.

Cory Stratton, epicenter of triumphal expectations, let himself listen to a tiny voice within: "What have I gotten myself into? Oh, well, if you can't retreat it's better to advance." He brought his wife and chidren center stage to share a group hug. This moment was featured on all major daily newspapers the following day, in the opening minutes of the evening news broadcasts, and shown on the most-watched internet video loop.

Dreams are the seeds for a new and better reality.

# Other Site, Other Outcome

EDWARD GALWAY'S CONVENTION was held in Pittsburgh, Pennsylvania on the 11th and 12th of August. It is important to note this fact because when the time came for the selection of the incumbent President and Vice President as their party's nominees for these same posts the event was designated as a "below the fold" news item. The nation's read-worthy newspapers, the tabloids, and the television, radio and internet news reports during the time of the Convention had their attention sharply focused on two developing stories occurring elsewhere. The lack of excitement in Pittsburgh did not help Galway's already difficult task of overcoming Cory Stratton's boost in the polls as a result of his inspirational acceptance address.

At home, the media was presenting the drama of the frantic evacuation of sections of the City of Los Angeles as a firestorm consumed vast tracts of land to the east. Climate change had been creeping into the national awareness since the start of the new Millenneum. In Southern California the issue became apparent when the sun-baked region experienced a drop in its already scant rainfall totals during the April to December period over the past several years. In the mountains bordering the city an average of less than 2 inches of rain was likely during the dry season. The vegatation that managed to sprout in the wet season (January through March) was drained of moisture in years when daily temperatures reached 100 degrees Fahrenheit at the beginning of April.

2008 was such a year—with an added catastrophic feature of an early appearance of the Santa Ana Winds. The Winds blow across Los Angeles from the east or northeast, having been created by a combination of a strong in-land high pressure system and a strong low pressure storm off the coast. The Winds usually began after September, but here it was mid-August and the Winds were gusting to 79 MPH.

Politics added to the problem. The Federalist-controlled Senate had not yet approved the President's nominee for Interior Secretary. This delayed formulation of the agency's budget prioritization—which meant no money was being spent on clearing away the tinder-dry vegatation in the mountains around the city.

On August 9th an unknown back-packer in the Angeles National Forest near Monrovia is believed to have neglected to effectively extinguish his camp fire. A spark was caught by the Winds and by mid-afternoon an inferno was devouring the landscape.

The waves of ash and smoke, the barrage of flaming debris, the clouds of lethal fumes and a rapidly advancing flame wall estimated at 300 feet high led one exhausted firefighter to remark: "It was like scenes from Peter Jackson's new trilogy, Pompeii." (The films were based on the 2003 novel by Robert Harris.)

By the 12th, over 480 square miles had been charred by the conflagration. Its advance towards the coast was halted at the Golden State Highway just east of Stars Stadium. Ninety-six people were reported as killed, most of these were civilians who had attempted to save their homes by using garden hoses. Five firefighters were killed when a flame-bomb exploded out of the inferno and struck a command post a mile away.

Downtown Los Angeles was a wasteland of smoke, ash and debris; a half-dozen major fires were started in the area by wind-blown embers. The overall economic cost of the calamity was later put at $10 billion. It was the most significant natural disaster within the United States since the December 16, 1947 earthquake that devastated St. Louis, Missouri. The 9.0 temblor severely damaged or destroyed over 50% of the structures in the city, and killed 1712 people.

\* \* \* \* \*

Further south a political storm was erupting. On Sunday August 10th Mexico held an election for President and members of the Chamber of Deputies. The incumbent President could not seek re-election. He had been the first opposition candidate ever elected to the post; and, now the Popular Revolutionary Movement (MPR) was seeking to regain control of the top political office.

The two major opposition parties again agreed upon a coalition and a joint candidate. The campaign process was being monitored by representatives of the Organization of Western Hemisphere States (OWHS).

Mexico's disaster struck late Sunday night. The popular vote count had reached a point where the observers were on the verge of declaring the coalition's Presidential candidate (university professor Eduardo de Valera Costilla) the victor. Shortly after 11PM an explosion rocked the building housing the tabulation center, knocking out the electricity and communications systems. Then, troops armed with assault rifles and flash lights entered the center and forced everyone out onto the streets. The commander of these troops based within the city had been appointed by the last MPR President, and he was still loyal to the organization.

At the stroke of midnight a MPR spokesman announced that the "official" vote count had been completed. It showed the MPR's candidate had received 49.8% of the vote to de Valera's 48.9%. The remaining votes were scattered among several minor candidates. The results for the Chamber of Deputies were not included in the statement.

The coalition parties and the OWHS observers were outraged. Their protests were given the stage of immediate access to news crews from around the world. Mr. de Valera was scopped up by the correspondent for World Network News, and was provided a full hour to present his case to the planet. Most middle and upper class homes in Mexico City had access to international news reports. The coalition parties deployed sound trucks throughout the working class and poor sections warning of the MPR's blatant attempt to steal another election. By sunrise a huge throng had assembled in the Plaza de la Constitucion. Around 9AM de Valera and other prominent coalition leaders arrived to address the people. They declared that the independent observers would refute the MPR's claim, and that they were preparing to issue a report verifying de Valera as the President-elect.

When de Valera rose to speak the roar from those gathered was exhilarating as well as deafening. He proposed a march to the site of the Chamber of Deputies where he intended to request a proclamation of support from the current members. These Deputies' term in office would run until the results of the previous day's balloting could be verified. They would now be asked to decide on the legitimacy of the next Presidential Administration. A majority of those in the Chamber chosen at the previous election had been linked with the MPR; de Valera now hoped a vast public rally would sway those who feared the MPR was losing its iron grip. Mexico's Constitution, written by the founders of the MPR, did not provide a mechanism for resolving a disputed outcome. Such a development had been inconceivable within a MPR dominated system.

The debate in the Chamber began Monday afternoon. It rapidly decended into shrill-voiced pandemonium. MPR

Deputies openly accused de Valera of being a paid dupe of Wall Street bankers. After several hours of haranguing each other the majority leader prepared to end the debate by calling for a vote. Some MPR Deputies responded by unleashing chants of "Illegal" and "Traitor" before storming out of the session. However, not all the MPR members departed. Enough stayed to provide a quorum for the coalition parties.

The head of the coalition in the Chamber was selected as a new majority leader. He proposed, had seconded, and obtained approval of a declaration accepting Eduardo de Valera Costilla as the President-elect. The issue was not so easily resolved, as the next morning's newspapers revealed.

The Miami Herald warned: "Mexico At Brink of Civil War—25 of 31 State Governors (all of MPR) Reject de Valera Vote By Deputies."

The Washington Post reported: "MPR Says Presidential Vote Is Null and Void."

The N.Y. Herald Tribune revealed: "Durango Drug Cartel Sees Gain in Turmoil—Danger of Colombia-Style Coup Feared."

The Tribune's article went to recall the events which led to the cancellation of Colombia's 1992 Presidential election. The South American nation had been traumatized for decades by an escalating torrent of violence. Historically, this strife was a blood-feud between political extremes. In the 1980s a third faction, the country's powerful drug cartel, entered the fray. Within a decade the cartel dominated nearly a third of Colombia.

In 1992 four candidates were assassinated during the Presidential campaign, including a reform-minded Senator who had been projected as the probable winner by several polls. Six weeks before Election Day an Army General, long believed by the U.S. Drug Enfocement Agency to be on the payroll of the cartel, staged a coup d'etat and ousted the incumbent, democratically elected Government. The General declared his actions were intended to defend the State against chaos created by "undisciplined civilians." He pledged to restructure the political process and return the government to a democratic format "when an appropriate scenario evolved." The General complimented this announcement with the appointment of several known drug traffickers to Cabinet posts. Sixteen years later the General still occupies the Presidential palace.

\* \* \* \* \*

Edward Galway's acceptance speech was summarized in a 15-second sound bite on most of Tuesday's late evening broadcast news programs. Articles on the closing ceremonies were bumped back in many of Wednesday's (the 13th) newspapers and news web-sites. Far more attention was being lavished upon the devastation in California.

President Galway departed Pittsburgh shortly after delivering his speech, and headed for the West Coast. His campaign staff hoped the opportunity for Galway to display the power of the Presidency, by announcing the details of a Federal relief effort, would bolster the voters' opinion of him. Galway was scheduled to make a walking tour of downtown Los Angeles at 3:30 PM Wednesday. However, the fire and the Santa Ana Winds were still forces to be reckoned with. Galway was required to spend Wednesday in Sacramento, the State Capital—over 350 miles away, waiting for the situation to clear around Los Angeles. The highways and train lines leading to L.A. were impassable, and the Winds made flying too risky for the Secret Service's comfort.

Meanwhile, local and national news crews were showing the Mayor of Los Angeles, a supporter of Cory Stratton, visiting neighborhood after neighborhood in her devastated city—all while wearing a jacket with the phrase "Let's Get To Work!" emblazoned on the back. The Mayor encouraged people by telling them everything would be re-built with the help of an actual leader in Washington.

When Galway finally arrived on Thursday evening the

ceremony was very low key. The Mayor sent her regrets, and an Assistant Deputy Commissioner of Tourism, citing the urgent nature of her duties to the citizens of the city. The proposed walking tour never materialized. President Galway finally made his announcement of Federal disaster relief on Friday morning before a breakfast meeting of local party stalwarts.

# *Autumn: A Time To Harvest Votes*

By Labor Day Cory Stratton had opened up a 15-percentage point lead in several major opinion polls. The central theme of Stratton's Fall campaign was to reinvigorate the concept of "government FOR the people." He pledged his commitment to extensive campaign finance overhaul, a wide-ranging reform of immigration legislation, the establishment of a permanent and independent Integrity Oversight Commission, and procuring a "cease-fire" with Congress on partisan acrimony on the key domestic issues of job creation with a living wage, equal rights, education and health care. Along with this announcement Stratton released a signed and witnessed pledge that he would not seek re-election if these four goals had not been achieved.

When President Galway was questioned concerning Stratton's pledge he dismissed it as game-playing. "While I thank Mr. Stratton for supporting basic concepts that I'm sure many Americans view favorably, his offer not to seek a second term is flawed on two points. First of all, I'm going to win in November; and, secondly, it's one of the oldest tricks in the book to make such an offer then abandon it later claiming revised circumstances. The problem with novices running for office is that they rely on cliches which any knowledgeable professional would distain."

In rebuttal Stratton replied: "I respect President Galway and the office he holds. But he will need to find new lodgings come next January. He shouldn't move too far away because I intend asking him in January 2012 whether or not I have kept my commitment to the American people."

\* \* \* \* \*

The four televised debates between Galway and Stratton adhered to a style of exchange whereby the President sought to project an air of executive authority through reflective and sober rejoinders, while the former Joint Chiefs Chairman achieved this goal by employing an expressive delivery of concise, thoughtful proposals. Stratton projected the image of one who was tired of the-same-old-same-old. Galway based his entire political life on supporting the status quo, without its hidebound rules and concepts his cue cards would be blank.

By the time the World Series ended on the last Sunday in October (the 26th), with the National Conference Havana Sugar Canes having defeated the American Conference Washington Senators, Stratton's lead was up to 20-percentage points. The voting on Election Day, November 4th, confirmed in graphic detail what Edward Galway had known for a month; his time in office would end on January 20, 2009. It was not only a bad day for an incumbent executive, but also a bad day for incumbent legislators. Beginning early in the year present Members began falling by the waste side as voters, heeding Cory Stratton's calls for a national renewal, began ousting long-term residents of Congress. Nearly 25% of all Congressional incumbents who sought re-election suffered defeat either in a primary or in the general election. For the first time since 1936 the number of third-party candidates selected to the House of Representatives reached double digits (14).

Cory Stratton enjoyed a tremendous day. The signs of his landslide triumph were apparent by the early evening exit polls. He went on to obtain 61% of the popular vote, with an extraordinary turnout for the U.S. of 65.1%. This was the highest turnout in literally a century—the 1908 election had a 65.4% participation level. Stratton won 522 of the 543 Electoral College votes. Edward Galway managed to carry only his own home State of Pennsylvania. Stratton's adopted political party maintained its majorities in the House and Senate; the Federalists had regained control of the House in the 2006 mid-term election. The influx of new recruits, who would look to Stratton rather than the traditional leadership structure for direction, promised exciting times for reporters and headaches for policy forecasters.

President Galway telephoned Stratton at his campaign headquarters at Brooklyn's Marriott Hotel shortly after 11 PM.

"Well, Cory...oh...I should say Mr. President-elect. Congratulations. It looks like I will be taking orders from you in the near future."

"Thank you, Mr. President," replied Stratton. "You will have to excuse my hoarse voice. I've done a bit more yelling than usual. It's rather noisy here."

"I can imagine," Galway said stiffly.

"Will we be able to meet soon? The world seems determined to intrude on our awareness," Stratton inquired.

"My people will call your people in the morning. One good thing about our post-election procedures is that it doesn't force the poor, misunderstood incumbent to pack his bags immediately. I look forward to seeing you. Again, congratulations."

# The Fuse Is Lit

ANY THOUGHTS, or hopes, held by Edward Galway of fading away easily did not make it to the end of the year, never mind the end of his term.

An election in a long-established democracy is meant to be the peaceful resolution of a current round of policy debates. The plebiscite held in the Canadian Province of Quebec on Tuesday November 18th was a sharp exception. Generations of mistrust and misunderstanding between French- and English-speaking residents had slowly brewed into a tempest. Outsiders considered it bizarre that long-term neighbors would suddenly lose all restraint and contemplate violent action for no other reason than each spoke a different primary language.

The question at hand was whether Quebec should separate from the Canadian Confederation and proclaim itself an independent nation. Many English-speakers had decided flight was indeed preferable to fight since the previous ballot on the Province's future. This altered the balance of power sufficiency to enable the Separatists to eke out a narrow win. The "Yes" (or more precisely, "Oui") vote was 50.01%.

The Federal Government in Ottawa assumed the Separatists

would soon request a negotiations conference. There was still an expectation in Prime Minister Paul Jennings' office that a compromise could be achieved. Such hope died when Quebec officials posted armed guards at all major "border points," removed all Maple Leaf flags displayed in public, and banned the use of English in official transactions. Any questions from the news media asked in English were ignored.

A serious problem became a crisis when an unidentified gang of thugs went on a rampage in downtown Montreal. One English-speaking tourist was stabbed to death. The PM's request to Quebec's Premier to allow the Canadian National Police to investigate the crime was denied. This prompted a call from a parliamentary Member representing a district in British Columbia. The Member, Wayne Stanley, belonged to the Cascadia Party; this organization believed it was far past due to shed the last taints of colonialism. It wanted to rename British Columbia, changing it to Cascadia.

In an open letter to Prime Minister Jennings, Mr. Stanley called for a resolution denouncing the murder of a Canadian citizen by Quebec criminals. The proposal went on to state that if Quebec authorities did not immediately apprehend and surrender the murderers to Federal prosecutors then the Quebec regime would be considered in breech of Canadian law. Mr. Stanley recommended that if such a finding were made it would be the Prime Minister's legal obligation to dispatch Federal troops to restore the rule of Canadian law.

The PM did not respond to this letter. In Quebec's reaction the Government said the letter was a perfect example of the anti-French hysteria rampant throughout Anglo-Canada. Several large and boisterous demonstrations were conducted in the Province calling upon France and the League of Nations to help protect Quebec's independence from "foreign-based threats."

A step back from the brink was taken when Quebec's Premier, Pierre Montesquieu, announced that suspects had been arrested. He said "this internal matter is no longer of concern to outsiders." The Premier called upon Ottawa to begin negotiations to "resolve any technical matters resulting from Quebec's lawful separation from the Confederation." The chief matter at hand became the closing of the border between the Province and Canada. Quebec officials were requiring anyone seeking entrance from Canada to produce a passport and visa. However, Quebec had not yet created a visa form or an application to request a visa. For the time being all traffic was being routed through an openly used, and openly over-looked, back door through the United States.

Wayne Stanley did not feel slighted by the silence from the PM's office. He had made his point. Westerners would now realize that the Ottawa-based Government was once again coddling Quebec. The time was coming when the West would awake and no longer care what the Easterners did, he said to himself.

\* \* \* \* \*

The Galway Administration, in its waning days, took no position on the question of Quebec other than to urge both sides to resolve their differences peacefully. Some problems can be settled by negotiations; others are devised and constructed by those who seek nothing but mayhem. This is what the United States was faced with in Acapulco, Mexico starting on New Year's Day 2009.

Three and a half years earlier a violent storm had devastated much of Acapulco's poorly constructed working-class neighborhoods. The city's line of beach-front tourist hotels was barely inconvenienced. For many guests the most significant consequence had been that they were required to use the indoor, heated pools rather than swim in the ocean. The surf was contaminated by overflow from the city's flooded sewer system. Despite a visit by the President, local authorities had done little in the interval to rebuild the city. The shattered lives of the residents did, however, draw the attention of a regional drug kingpin. He provided jobs within his organizatio for some, to others he made loans available (at horrendous interest rates); but, most of all he maintained a stream of propaganda against the foreigners who flaunted their wealth in the face of unrelenting hardship.

Acapulco's Hilton Hotel was at 70% capacity. The ongoing political turmoil had persuaded a notable portion of the Hotel's regular New Year's patrons to find the Sun elsewhere. Eduardo de Valera Costilla had been sworn in as President before a joint session of Mexico's Congress. The political structure remained divided. The MPR members of the newly-elected Congress, now a minority, were conducting a boycott. They were demanding that de Valera resign so that a new election (without outside observers) could be held. Most State Governors, including the Governor of Guerrero where Acapulco is located, were MPR members. Their opposition to de Valera was intense. Anything that could undercut him would be beneficial to the MPR, so the Governors' reactions to any event were motivated accordingly.

Chiming bells, popping champagne corks and a Mariachi band greeted the New Year for the Hotel's guests. The main ballroom was crowded with approximately 250 revelers, mostly Americans. At first the shouting did not penetrate the din of celebration. Those furthermost away from the main entrance assumed some other party-goers had been over-indulging already, despite the early hour. Everyone's attention was grabbed by the neck when bursts of automatic weapons fire ripped into the ceiling.

Standing at every doorway and window were heavily armed masked men. They all wore dark combat uniforms. Each held an assault rifle pointed towards the crowd. Their commander shouted in Spanish, then English, "Men to my right, women to my left, and all your jewels, cash, credit cards and cell phones on the floor in the middle. If you hold anything back you will be shot after we kill your companion." Compliance was panicky but swift. Within twenty minutes the raiders had secured the building and telephoned the

Mayor's home. A ransom demand of $1 million American for each hostage was made. The gunmen, who were later identified as cohorts of the local drug kingpin, also demanded a passenger jet. Once the ransom was delivered the hostages would be released—after the gunmen, the hostages and the money had flown safely to Bogota, Colombia. If these demands were not accepted within 24 hours two hostages would be thrown from the roof of the hotel each hour until the terms were accepted.

The city's Police Commander sent the few officers he had available to the hotel. This was mainly to prevent anyone else from entering the building and being taken prisoner. The Commander telephoned the Governor's office; however, a recorded message revealed the facility was closed until the following week. Guests from other hotels were drawn to the scene by the arriving police cars. When they learned of the hostage-taking several called the American Embassy on their cell phones. By 2 AM the U.S. Ambassador was advising President Galway of what little he knew.

"Well, Henry. What can you tell me?"

"Not very much, Mr. President. I have several key aides headed for the hotel. It appears that over 200 U.S. citizens are being held by drug-gang terrorists. They're demanding $1M per in ransom. The local cops aren't much help. Most of the authorities for the area are off on vacation; and the President is trying to hold the country together. The station chief has some disturbing background data on the local Governor. It's nothing we can present in court, but it gives us real trouble if true."

"We're not at the point of legal proceedings, Henry. Tell me what the Spook thinks he knows," said the President.

Hesitating a moment the Ambassador replied, "The Governor is probably on the cartel's payroll. An informer claims the Governor and the area's narcolord are pals from way back. A lot of money, and consumable commodities, have passed between them over the years. The Governor apparently was crying in his beer lately about how his privileges were being curtailed by de Valera. He told his drinking buddy something big was needed to pressure de Valera into being 'realistic.' This outrage may be the outcome of that conversation."

Galway wondered aloud, "How much does the Mexican Government know about this guy?"

"Everyone here believes everyone who is somebody in the MPR is on the take from one special interest group or another," replied the Ambassador. "Do you want me to provide de Valera with our background info?"

"Not right now," the President answered. "I'm sending you two dozen FBI Agents and some technical folks with Delta Force. We can't make an overt display until we're certain the central Government will accept our assistance. When will you meet with de Valera?"

"As soon as I conclude..." In the background a voice was telling the Ambassador to switch on his television set. Simultaneously, a Presidential aide was entering the Oval Office. WNN was broadcasting a special report.

* * * * *

"...newsroom. Again, our breaking story—Terror in Paradise. As we have been reporting, a large number of vacationers at the Hilton Hotel in Acapulco, Mexico were seized by terrorists shortly after midnight. We have just learned that several people who were in the Hilton tried to escape. They were fired upon by the gunmen. We are told that at least six people were hit. We do not know yet the extent of their injuries. One of the wounded is still on the ground outside the hotel. Civilians outside the hotel attempting to rescue the individual were driven back by heavy gunfire... Recapping our story..."

"Oh, my God!" Galway moaned. "Henry! Are you there?"

"Yes, Mr. President."

"Get to President de Valera immediately! He must send his own specialists in as soon as practical. Discuss our request for deployment. Tell him we understand their sensitivity on the matter."

"I'm on my way, Sir. I'll report back ASAP."

\* \* \* \* \*

President-elect Cory Stratton was kept well-informed on all the public and behind the scenes developments. His comments to the news media were limited to expressing his concern for the hostages and acknowledging that President Galway faced a difficult situation.

Stratton knew that several anti-terrorist and special warfare units had been authorized to prepare, but within U.S. territory. A hostage negotiation team, comprising Mexican and American experts, was in constant communication with the gunmen. Sixty-four people, either women or elderly men, were released within a few days; and, the terrorists had not carried out their retaliation threat for non-compliance with their demand for money. As the standoff proceeded into its second week the hostage-takers seemed to be settling in for a long haul. The Hilton was well stocked, and only the bare minimum needed to be shared with the victims.

Stratton announced at this time that all Inauguration Day festivities (the parade, the dinner parties and the midnight balls) were cancelled. "This nation is caught up in a tragedy. We can all celebrate when these brave Americans come home in good health," he said at a press conference. On January 20th Cory Stratton took the Oath of Office on the western steps of the Capitol Building. In a tense address to the American public President Stratton pledged that the United States Government would achieve a successful resolution of the "cowardly criminal scenario in Acapulo." When he met with the Joint Chiefs of Staff later in the day the President said, "I might just re-enlist so I can be in on the resolution." The military commanders were only somewhat certain that the President's remark was not serious.

A considerable amount of additional preparation began by nightfall on the 20th. The Pentagon had already achieved a higher level of preparedness than outlined by the prior Administration (based on the Joint Chiefs' belief that the new National Command Authority would support a robust counter-action); when President Stratton said "go" U.S. forces were not starting from square one. Virtually none of this activity was visible to the public. President Stratton in a series of telephone calls to key figures in the media constructed a wall of silence around the developing rescue operation. The media was offered complete background information on the condition that nothing be released until after the situation had been resolved.

On January 28th all was ready. A U.S. naval task force arrived off the coast of Acapulco. A helicopter carrier held an array of troop-carrying craft for deploying special warfare units and transferring out rescued civilians. An aircraft carrier was to be the launching pad of the task force's striking power.

The previous night a commando team had infiltrated the hotel, making their way to the fifth floor (where the women were being held) and the sixth floor (where the men were held). Four commandos went to each of these locations and hid, waiting for the attempt. Altogether there were three dozen gunmen in the building. Most were on the ground floor, with a dozen spread among the hostage groups. A handful was stationed on the roof as lookouts. Various helicopters had been flying above the city, at all hours, for the previous ten days; therefore, when four large choppers swept across the sky at 2 AM the lookouts did not pay them undue attention. The craft went past the hotel and headed in-land. A rumble of thunder, or so it seemed, came from the ocean. In fact, the noise was generated by four ground-support A-10 Warthogs from the U.S. Air Force. Strapped under their wings were precision-guided stun bombs. They flew in from the sea, with their targets set as the Hilton's ground floor and roof.

When the lookouts turned towards the sound of the planes the helicopters landed and discharged 50 soldiers. Before any warning could be given a stun bomb from an A-10 exploded in the midst of the lookouts. The terrorists on the ground floor were caught in a cross-fire of such devices, which crashed in through all the windows. On the floors above hostages and gunmen were jolted as concussions rocked the structure. The American commandos emerged from hiding and efficiently dispatched the disorganized terrorists.

The ground floor was soon swarming with the newly arrived troopers, who wasted little time arguing with any gunman witless enough to resist surrender. No hostages were injured, and only half a dozen members of the rescue force sustained injuries. Of the terrorists three were killed, while most of the others received various injuries in the assault.

Additional troops and helicopters arrived shortly, and by noon all of the former hostages had been transported to either of the carriers stationed off-shore. The commanding officer of the task force notified the Mexican officials who arrived at the Hilton that all of the terrorists were in American custody and would be brought to the U.S. for trial. Some officials attempted to protest citing jurisdiction to no avail. President Stratton met all the rescued holiday-makers two days later at a reception in Washington.

Mexico faded from the headlines as February progressed into March. Yet the underlying social turmoil was taking a toll on the nation. People desparate to escape the poverty, crime and corruption spawned by the MPR era had for years been flooding into the southwestern corner of the United States. President de Valera sought to bring about reform, but the lingering influence of the MPR fought him every step of the way. However, as an institution, the MPR was beginning to disassemble. It had long been held together by a network of patronage, graft and strong-arm threats. The party's loss of the Presidency and Congress was a further weakening of its control of local bosses. Three of the six

Mexican States bordering the U.S. were nominally MPR-held. In reality these States were controlled by offshoots of the Durango cartel specializing in smuggling drugs and people across the border. Local mayors on the U.S. side were demanding that the Stratton Administration declare a state of emergency and seal the border with Federal soldiers. The volume of refugees had dipped for a while immediately after de Valera's inauguration, but the hostage drama stirred fears of further violence. Entire families were a common sight among the renewed surge of desperate people seeking entrance to America, one way or another.

A rapid-response shuttle service developed as U.S. immigration officers detained a growing percentage of this human tide, and returned them to Mexico on an expedited basis. In turn, Mexican security officials established transit camps for the returnees. The Government did not want to simply put them back on the street fearing these individuals would just head for the border once more. Opposition to the camps came not only from the detainees and civil rights organizations but also from the smugglers. If the Government persuaded people not to flee there would be a substantial drop-off on the gang's steady income. On several occasions the smugglers attempted to stage a break-out from the camps. While a few people managed to get out most were deterred by the gun battles that erupted between camp guards and smugglers. In response to such tactics President de Valera proposed, and the Congress quickly passed, a "Prevention of Potential Risk" statute. This measure allowed any prosecutor to declare a known criminal as a potential risk, thereby permitting the preventive detention of the suspect. Evidence of past or potential illegal activity, or credible supposition of such potential illegal activity, would then be presented to a judge on a special Federal review panel. If the judge concurred the suspect would be held without bail (or further charges) for six months. At such time the prosecutor could ask for an extension. Civil rights organizations denounced the law, but the Government contended it would only be used against professional criminals. An expected legal challenge would take time to wind its way through the court system; until then the Government was prepared to make full use of the provision.

The cartel expressed its defiance very blatantly. One of the key centers in the smuggling network was the city of Tijuana, in the State of Baja California Norte. The Governor of the State belonged to the anti-MPR coalition. He was a strong supporter of President de Valera and the preventive detention law. On the morning of May 15th the Governor was visiting Tijuana to inspect improvements to a transit center damaged in a break-out attempt a few weeks earlier. As he stepped out of his car, which was parked in front of the camp's administrator's office, a series of dull thuds could be heard. Seconds later mortar shells rained down on the car. The Governor and seven people standing nearby were killed instantly; eighteen other people were wounded.

Another series of mortar shells crashed onto the gateway, opening a sizable gap. Swarms of detainees were soon running out of the camp, and blocking all rescue and medical teams from entering. The American city of San Diego is not far away. Frantic telephone calls were made by the city's Mayor and the Governor of California to the White House demanding immediate help. The Mayor wanted President Stratton to dispatch an Army division to seal the border near the city. Stratton responded by issuing an order placing California's National Guard under Federal control. These units were then deployed to assist the already in-place Border Patrol officers; the President augmented the Patrol by transferring 100 officers from other sections of the country. An expected surge of refugees did not materialize. Yet politicians and community groups in the four American States bordering Mexico were sending a continuing, and ever more frantic, message to Washington that a long-term solution was needed before a critical scenerio became a catastrophe.

Not to be outdone in this hour of pathos, Canada reasserted itself into the limelight. June 24th, the feast day of John the Baptist—the patron Saint of Quebec—had long been an occasion of patriotic fervor in the Province. With its move towards separatism the day became a focal point in Quebec's political crisis. Following the December plebiscite the Provincial leadership initially spoke of independence, but later claimed they had not formally declared where the area stood in relationship with Anglo-Canada. They referred to the results as an acknowledgement of the people's expectation for change. The leaders thought, or hoped, the outcome would spark major concessions by Ottawa. While the Parti Kebec had long demanded separation a detailed plan of action for implementing such action had never been finalized.

Both sides now waited for the other to blink while they both had their eyes shut.

Fearful of more militant adherents of his Parti Kebec, Premier Pierre Montesquieu finally decided it was time to decide. At a huge rally on June 24th in Quebec City the Premier formally declared Quebec to be a free and independent nation. He said Quebec would apply for membership in the League of Nations, the Organization of Western Hemisphere States and the North American Free Trade Association. He called upon France and the United States to act as guarantors of Quebec's freedom against "any and all foreign encroachments." Canada's Prime Minister, Paul Jennings, revealed his "sorrow" concerning Quebec's "hasty reaction." He called for further negotiations between the two societies.

July 1st, the day set aside to celebrate the establishment of the Canadian Confederation, had long not been an occasion of patriotic fervor. A conference in Vancouver sought to have the day observed in a different manner. Having privately warned PM Jennings of their exhausted patience on the matter of Quebec, the Premiers of Alberta, British Columbia, Manitoba and Saskatchewan now went public with their displeasure. They scolded Jennings for his lack of assertiveness towards Quebec. They chastised Quebec's politicians as grand-standing brats. They outlined their responsibilities to the people of their own Provinces, and questioned whether Ottawa was capable of assisting in such obligations. They declared their opposition to any further negotiation unless it was for the sole purpose of re-setting the Confederation. If such a proposal was not unequivocally accepted by Ottawa and Quebec by the end of the month the four Premiers stated they would consider the Confederation irrevocably terminated.

"How can we be party to a nation where the central government refuses to uphold its own laws? How can we be equal partners with a Province that considers equality to be a betrayal of a 'special relationship' it wants but won't define? We cannot drag our people, the People of The Northern Prairie (a name highlighted in the official press release), down a road of ceaseless political turmoil. If the national partnership does not work—let's admit it and move on!"

The Premiers would not answer any questions from the assembled reporters concerning what they had in mind if Ottawa and Quebec did not favorably respond by August 1st.

What the Premiers had in mind was known to Alex Poller. He was now Chief of Staff to America's Vice President, Bert Maurus. On the evening of July 1st Poller and Maurus had dinner at the former Governor's home near Columbus, Ohio. Poller was vacationing there for the Independence Day holiday. After the meal the men adjourned to Maurus' study while his family went outside to watch a fireworks display.

"Thanks again for inviting me, Bert. It's always a pleasure meeting Celeste and the kids," Poller said as they settled into armchairs before a bay window.

"Well, Al, it gives you a chance to see how the other half lives. You know, people who don't spend 27 hours a day in search of intrigue can lead fulfilling lives," the Vice President replied in a friendly jab at his non-stop aide.

"You may be sorry that I can't work full-time once you hear the latest," laughed Poller. "The Canadian Premiers are finally coming around. You'll remember that I met with them last year for a preliminary review. They were hesitant then, but events have pulled them towards our viewpoint."

Maurus asked, "Have you had any recent discussions?"

"They expressed-mailed a copy of their statement of earlier today before it went public. The document did not come directly from any of their offices, so for now our contacts are unofficial," Poller replied.

"How far are they willing to come? Do they expect anything from us?" inquired the Vice President.

Poller stood up and gazed out the window for a moment. Then said, "They're willing to let Jennings dither away the Confederation. He won't rap knuckles or knock heads together to save his country. He'd make a lousy hockey player. Too damn Anglo for his own good. I think its time for you, Mr. Vice President, to begin laying the foundation for a formal Administration policy statement. We have to direct the President's thoughts towards a favorable view on this subject. You can present it as the act of a good neighbor."

Returning to the chair, Poller continued, "Everything that has happened so far has been totally Canadian in origin... more or less. No one can find our DNA on anything. We must now take a more direct approach. Our point should be that America is willing to assist a valiant people who suddenly find themselves cut adrift. If they should request more than neighborly good wishes so much the better."

"The President needs to be alerted to this possibility. We don't want him to spout off some Boy Scout dribble about non-interference. He has to be shown that America's territorial growth need not be discussed merely in the past tense. We are the New World. We have done more with it, for more people than any other nation. Our neighbors were lucky to hold together this long. Instability is now the number one threat to peace. West Asia and its zealots are the prime example. We must be pro-active in our response to instability on our doorstep."

With a clap of hands Maurus replied, "Nice little speech. Who said you're no more than a henchman? The President will be at 1600 all next week. He's considering a full Cabinet meeting on the topic of our neighbors before he goes off on vacation to the Adirondacks. Prepare your ideas as talking points for me. Make only one copy. Don't save it on a PC or anything else. We can't have copies floating around cyperspace."

"I know how to delete files, Bert. I'm not one of those intern trolls who work in the basement. As you insist, I'll resort to quill and ink," answered Poller. "Next week we light the fuse. The fireworks bang will come a little later." Other fuses were being lit. Other explosions were coming sooner.

\* \* \* \* \*

If Americans like anything most of all its long holiday weekends—especially in the Summer. The 4th of July 2009 fell on a Saturday. Gone was the era when this meant a one-day celebration. Casual Fridays had become Casual Half-Day Fridays, and Thursday at noon was now considered the unofficial beginning of the weekend getaway for many. This Independence Day was to be a multiple day event, with a noticeable number of workers and executives taking an extended number of personal days.

Mexico's Durango drug cartel saw this corruption of the work ethic as something they could exploit. Border guards are people too, and the infectious idea of a mega-weekend would enter their minds as well. Especially those unfortunate souls stuck working the late shift on July 4th night. A branch of the cartel planned a major run of drugs and people across the border into Texas that night. Boredom and resentment were seen as aids in dulling the sentries' alertness.

A joint Border Patrol-Texas Rangers unit, operating out of Laredo, was patrolling a desolate region northwest of the city. Two all-terrain vehicles, each with five men inside, bounced over the landscape headed for an oft-used transit route. A helicopter was available for an overhead view if contact was made. Each member of the unit was equipped with night-vision goggles to cut down on any advantage the moonless sky offered. Around midnight a member of the unit transmitted a message to HQ that a convoy of trucks had been spotted. The unit was advancing and requested that the chopper move up to their GPS co-ordinates.

When the craft arrived the crew witnessed the end stage of a firefight. Their call for back-up was abruptly curtailed. Within a half an hour 40 additional heavily-armed officers were on the scene. They could do nothing to aid their companions, except initiate a bitter manhunt. Twelve Americans had been killed defending their homeland's border. The ground unit had run into a hailstorm of assault weapons fire and a barrage of RPGs (rocket-propelled grenades). Three cartel vehicles had made the run; one contained drugs, another held people and the lead truck carried well-armed escorts. An unknown number of gunmen piled out of that vehicle to confront the patrol. Some of the Americans never made it out of their SUV. If any gunman was hit the others probably carried him away. The in-coming fire was too intense and unexpected by the Americans. The patrol managed to get off only a few rounds, and had no time to warn the two-man chopper crew. When the helicopter came on the scene it was knocked down by a gunman using a hand-held ground-to-air missile launcher. The cartel's convoy continued on its way, not choosing to wait for another encounter.

At 5 AM on July 5th President Stratton, Vice President Maurus and all 14 members of the Cabinet met in an emergency session at the White House. The Laredo tragedy was the sole topic of discussion. As they urgently settled in around the large oval table in the Cabinet Room the kitchen staff delivered mugs of coffee or tea and glasses of fruit juice for the attendees.

The President began the meeting with a moment of silent prayer for those murdered the previous night. He then said, "Thank you all for coming here so early. If it's any consulation I've been up since two talking with the JCS Chief and FBI Director Bernice Smyth and also President de Valera. There is a team of senior military officers and FBI Agents on their way to Mexico City to meet with their counterparts. I plan to go to Laredo myself tomorrow to meet members of our security forces there. President de Valera will join me later in Brownsville. We will discuss enhanced co-ordination of our border patrols."

The Vice President broke in to inject his comments. "I'm sure that I speak for everyone here, Mr. President, when I say—respectfully- that you should chew de Valera's head off. This outrage is further evidence that Mexico's days as an organized society are numbered. We can't rely on their security operatives; you've read the same OSS assessments I have. From crossing guards to the General Staff, corruption is pandemic. Whether it's Durango, the MRP or a freelance hood, money is flowing over and under the table. The only people we can rely on to safeguard our borders are our own guys and gals of the U.S. military. If it means ignoring a line on a map—let's make that decision now and get on with the job!"

"Mr. President," said Secretary of Defense Denise Thomas (Lt. Gen. U.S. Army, retired), "I can understand the Vice President'a passion in light of last night's horrendous events, but I hope he is not seriously advocating an incursion against a sovereign ally."

"Well, General," replied the President, "there are people in this country who would probably agree with Mr. Maurus" (who began a smile which didn't last) "but, I'm not one of them. Bert, if we go crashing across the border on a bandit-hunt it's likely to make things worse. Military operations take detailed planning. Moreover, there must be a clear objective along with a dedicated policy commitment to achieve attainable goals. What would you have us do? Venture in five miles? And if we could find an obvious narco-gunman and he pulls back ten miles, do we keep chasing him? The Mexicans will begin to view us as the problem, not the cartel."

The Vice President, making scant effort to disguise his annoyance, responded, "We cannot just sit on our butts and do nothing. Talking to the Mexes may soothe their egos, however it's not providing security to Americans. How do we tell the families of our murdered men that the United States of America is not going to take righteous action because it might offend the sensibilities of some bribe-taking incompetent foreigner?"

"Mr. President, Sir." It was the Secretary of Energy, a former Congressman from Houston. "In a way I do agree with the basic sentiment of the Vice President's remarks. American soil, Texas land I might add, has been violated and soaked with the blood of some of our brave men. People are fed up with criminals being pampered by lawyers who think prosecutors violate their clients' rights by upholding the law. International murderers are not different. Murder is murder. We can't allow it to go unpunished! What do you think de Valera will do, can do? What does he control other than the room he sits in? It's time for the posse to saddle up and ride out."

"Frank, I intend to have a very explicit discussion with President de Valera. I have spoken to him by phone prior to this tragedy. He is straightforward and determined to reform his society. We need his assistance in this endeavor. The Mexican Government realizes it's in a battle for its very own survival. This nest of thugs seeks to become the dominant power. The cartel has no respect for law. Yet we cannot defend the law by breaking it. The United States will have an appropriate and co-ordinated response with the de Valera Government."

"In addition," said the Secretary of State, "I will be meeting with the Foreign Ministers at an OWHS conference the President will call for later today. This type of terrorism is a hemispheric concern. We will obtain the in-put and support of our neighbors in dealing with the crisis."

"Twelve Americans are dead, Mr. Secretary!" shot back Maurus. "We don't need permission from anyone to defend ourselves. Talk isn't going to bring these assassins to justice. I hope this Administration is not going to be as inept as the previous two on foreign policy. Danger is at our doorsteps. Mexico is not the only border issue. We must be prepared to respond to developments in Canada which..."

"Whoa!" snapped President Stratton. "Bert, you're getting way off the topic. Our priority is resolving the threat posed by the cartel. We will do that in partnership with the Mexican Government. Sec State assures me the Assistant Sec State for North America is in contact with Prime Minister Jennings. That's all. Their debate on the format of their governing style is Canada's internal business."

"Mr. President, we will miss a great..."

"Enough, Bert! We all have important work to do." Addressing the Cabinet members the President added, "I will appreciate it if you all can draft recommendations on how your Department can participate in dealing with the main and collateral issues related to Mexico. Please have your reply e-mailed to Ann by 9 AM tomorrow." Turning to Anna D'Florence, his Chief of Staff, the President said, "Then we can see what co-ordination efforts can be implemented."

"Yes, Mr. President. If all the reports are in on time I'll have an analysis prepared for you by start of business Tuesday," the former insurance industry executive replied.

"OK. I'll see everyone after I return," Stratton stated as he rose and the session concluded. The Cabinet members quickly departed with a minimum of chatter, after first stopping to shake hands with the President and offering him encouragement on his trip. Vice President Maurus remained seated for a few minutes then left in a stony silence.

* * * * *

"He insulted me in front of the entire Cabinet!" shouted a visibly irate Bert Maurus. "He asks for advice but ignores anyone who offers an independent view." Maurus was storming back and forth in his work office at the Naval Observatory, the official residence of America's Vice President. The main witness to this outburst was Alex Poller.

"Just because he had some shiny baubles on his G.I. Joe outfit doesn't give him the right to disrespect me. I am the Vice President of the United States of America. I represent a vitally important constituency in this country. He can't order me around like some damn junior grade lieutenant. He can talk gruff with me, yet what does he propose to do with the Mexes? He wants a nice chat! Americans are being murdered and he's letting the Foggy Bottom crowd handle our response. Does this guy know what he's doing?"

Poller did no more than listen as Maurus vented his spleen for the louder part of twenty minutes.

\* \* \* \* \*

Cory Stratton's conference with Eduardo de Valera took the form of a two-day mini summit. Day one was spent in Brownsville, Texas; and, the follow-up gathering occurred directly across the border in Matamoros, Mexico. The outcome was predictable, however the occasion enabled the two leaders to obtain a personal sense of each other and establish a friendship. Stratton's Brooklyn-acquired knowledge of Spanish helped, with only limited need for translation into the form de Valera was aquainted with.

A joint task-force of military, security and judicial officials was established to oversee the response to the cartel's threat. A reward of $1,000,000 was offered for information leading to the capture of the leader of the Durango Cartel, who used the nom de guerre of El Guadana. Mexico would also begin a sizable sweep by its Army of a wide zone south of the border, with the intent of rooting out suspected cartel sites.

The MPR responded with accusations that de Valera planned to abrogate the Constitution and declare martial law. The party warned of military attacks against those who opposed de Valera. Mexico's President quickly and emphatically denied and denounced the accusations. He said the gravest threat to freedom was posed by the corruption spawned by the MPR.

One of the party's Governors, in control of the State of Sonora which borders Arizona, took it upon himself to "prove" the danger of de Valera's operation. The Governor had in his possession a supply of Mexican Army uniforms and weapons. A detachment of local police were provided with the gear and encouraged to conduct a bit of public disruption. The Governor hoped to embarrass de Valera, forcing him to curtail his alliance with the norte americanos. An ambitious police Captain thought he could expand on his mission, and reap a justifiable reward. The Captain and several of the men under his command did not survive their mission; nevertheless, they left behind grim evidence of the disastrous consequences of dangerous plots.

The ersatz troops, provided with reports on the patterns of the Mexican and American forces in the region, infiltrated Arizona during a brief window in the patrol coverage. The Captain's intention was to conduct a not-too-violent shoot-up of a small town, leaving a few tell-tale clues before vanishing into the countryside. He chose the town of Sasabe, which is just inside American territory. What he was unaware of as he approached the town was the presence of troopers from a U.S. Army platoon.

One of the platoon's Jeeps had the misfortune of engine trouble as it passed near Sasabe. The disabled vehicle was towed into the town, and the troops were awaiting the arrival of a mechanic.

Shortly after 11:30 PM local time on July 8th a line of trucks came rambling along the main street of Sasabe. The five transports stopped at irregular intervals and the ten "soldiers" in each one dismounted. They began firing into the air and towards the windows of darkened buildings. The few pedestrians nearby froze for a moment, then fled in terror. One had the presence of mind to make his way to where he had seen the troopers. A hurried, babbled account of marauding gunmen in military uniforms was enough for the Sergeant in charge to call in reinforcements; he had heard what sounded like gunfire earlier, but decided against taking action against what might only be some local yahoos.

The Sergeant was advised by a Major at his base to advance and obtain specific details. A helicopter gunship was on the way, he was told.

When the Sergeant and his men found the invaders they were standing in a cluster in the middle of the street. Their neglect to eliminate the street lights provided sufficient illumination for the Americans. The Sergeant shouted warnings in English and Spanish at the group, ordering them to put down their weapons. Several of the invaders made the fatal mistake of pointing their weapons towards the Americans. A fusillade from the troops ripped into the invaders. Only the gunmen farthest away escaped. They vanished into the night, leaving their trucks and comrades (9 dead, 15 wounded) behind. The Captain was among the fatalities.

Phoenix's Arizona Republic newspaper declared on its web site within the hour, and in an EXTRA edition published somewhat later:

**Sasabe Shoot Out!**
***U.S. Troops Repel Invaders!***
***Is War With Mexico Next?***

Details came from town residents who called the publication following the one-sided exchange. The Sergeant was interviwed by cell-phone before the Army could order those involved not to comment.

\* \* \* \* \*

The White House, the State Department and the office of Mexico's President spent the greater part of the following week in hyper-crisis management mode. When the remnants of the invaders were captured on July 10th by Arizona State Police (the survivors had turned north rather than south in their attempt to escape), they soon related to American authorities what little they knew about the planning of the mission. This, however, was sufficient for Mexican Federal Police to find a trail leading to the Sonora Governor. His body was found in a bedroom of his home. No note was discovered; the autopsy could not confirm whether the single gunshot wound to the head was self-inflicted or not.

In a background report published in the Columbus (Ohio) Dispatch a source, identified only as "close to the Administration" and speaking on condition of anonymity, was quoted as saying "there had been a sharp policy debate prior to Sasabe. A decision to delay a forceful response may have contributed to this tragedy. As a nation we are fortunate that no more American lives were lost to the lawless chaos emanating from Mexico. I don't know how long the U.S. public will stand for such a negligent lack of leadership."

The White House Press Secretary gave a terse "no comment" when asked about the report. Vice President Maurus' reaction to reporters' inquiries was the same as his reply to President Stratton, "I have no doubt that many citizens agree with that insightful statement. Simply because it was published in an Ohio newspaper doesn't mean I have to be responsible for putting it there."

\* \* \* \* \*

Cory Stratton did not pursue the question of responsibility for the time being; if for no other reason than it was drowned out by a rising chorus of public and Congressional demands for tougher action against the cartel. After consultations with de Valera, additional American and Mexican Army patrols began operating in cross-border joint maneuvers. To ease Mexican anxieties over the presence of American troops inside Mexico, Stratton gave his approval to allowing

Mexican troops to enter the United States. Both Presidents understood there was little chance of encountering a cartel base in the immediate area of the border. The troop movements were a show of force and a publicity event for the benefit of citizens and cartel alike.

Stratton was able to defuse the rhetoric on Capitol Hill chiefly through the efforts of the Congressional leadership, who were of course members of his party. It became increasingly difficult to realize that Bert Maurus was also a member of the President's party. Maurus had decided to stake out a position as irreconcilable advocate for a policy he labled "enhanced defensive deployment." He argued at Cabinet and National Security Council meetings that the U.S. needed to move beyond reacting to cartel outrages. At one Cabinet gathering the Vice President said, "By waiting for these thugs to show up, and expecting them to meekly surrender is absurd. Mexico's so-called government has not conclusively proved it can control its own flunkies, never mind the powerful Durango cartel. We have continuing reports of Mexican politicians obstructing the movement of their national troops. Smugglers are still infiltrating our borders from California to Texas. The tragedy of the capsized boat of refugees, apparently headed for Florida, is another example of Mexico's collapse. We cannot wait any longer as the problem comes to us. We need a buffer zone. A safeguard for our citizens. If de Valera's regime will assist us, so much the better. We should not, however, dismiss my proposal if the Mexes refuse to cooperate. Our obligations are to Americans, not to foreigners who can't control their own affairs."

President Stratton privately stated his opposition to such suggestions. His position went public when the Vice President, in direct confrontation to a warning by the President to keep his objections in-house, responded to a reporter's "How are you today?" question by launching into a bleak warning about American in-action concerning the cartel.

At a ceremony in the Oval Office for the visiting Italian

Premier, Tomas La Guidice, President Stratton warned that any attempt by the U.S. to occupy portions of Mexico would result in Americans being viewed as the threat. His voice of reason was applauded on the editorial pages, but the Vice President's sharp calls for dramatic action gained greater notice in the headlines, the evening news broadcasts, certain web-sites and (in particular) with the glib-tongued talk-meisters of satellite radio. By the end of August a noticeable segment of popular, Congressional and Cabinet opinion began creeping in the direction of Maurus' "enhanced defensive deployment."

\* \* \* \* \*

Not wishing for the planet to become enmeshed in just one crisis, Canada reasserted itself on August 15th. The Premiers of the Northern Prairie Provinces had issued a series of mild-mannered warnings after their initial deadline of August 1st had passed without action by the Ottawa Government. The Premiers now released a policy announcement which brought the nation past the point of possible dissolution. The divorce was presented in terms of abandonment, and a new arrangement was openly wished for.

A new nation-state government (the North Prairie Republic), formed by the collaboration of the four provincial governments, was declared. It viewed itself as being in external association with the Ottawa Government—for the time being. Co-operation would be maintained on social priority matters—food, fuel, transportation, communications and the like. However, political and taxation links were severed. The NPR chided Ottawa for reneging on its obligations, and reaffirmed its own commitment to the needs of the region's citizens. An acknowledgement was made to the difficulties the North Prairie Republic, as a mini-State, would face in a global market economy. A call was issued for interested parties to attend a conference scheduled for the following month. The Premiers of the NPR (the new government had a collective leadership) would then address the issue of a new strategic partnership. In response to reporters' inquiries the Premiers declared their willingness to consider any reasonable alliance, but stated it was not likely that a revised Canadian confederation could be formed. They also welcomed any interest the Yukon or Inuit territories would have in associating with the NPR. The four did admit, after repeated prodding by the reporters, that the most practical option would involve the United States.

# A White House Divided

WITHIN A WEEK Mexico had reclaimed the media spotlight. On August 21st a protest march by a few hundred demonstrators took place in Mexico City. The marchers called for an end to what they saw as an American invasion of their homeland. Their chants were appeals for the release of all "prisoners of war"; the captives in question were known members of the cartel. It was not until the crowd approached the American Embassy that any trouble occurred. The chants became rants. The appeals for freedom became accusations of war crimes. From somewhere in the gathering Molotov cocktails were hurled against the embassy's gate. Within a few minutes a large force of police came on the scene, and attempted to clear the street. The protestors refused to move, and sat down in defiance of an order to disperse. Moments later the crowd was scattering in panic. Shots had been fired and fighting erupted on the line where police and demonstrators met. An official inquiry later reported that there were too many conflicting accounts on the origins of the gunshots to reach a definitive conclusion. Although no one was reported hit, rumors swept the city within hours that two marchers had been killed. The police and the Americans were blamed and accused of having burned and hidden the bodies. The next day several thousands decended on the Embassy. Street-wide banners displayed calls for an end to American military intervention. Denunciations were made of the 19th Century conflict between the two countries and of Pershing's raids in the 20th Century. A double-wall of riot police stood guard around the Embassy, as armed Marines patrolled the inside grounds.

The American Ambassador and Mexico City's Mayor agreed to meet in front of the Embassy with the march organizers, and the family of those allegedly killed. The two officials assured the organizers that no one had been injured by gunfire the prior day. (No grieving relatives were on hand, and the march leaders could not provide any names or photos of the alleged victims.) The Ambassador said he had available videotape from security cameras scanning the area. The tapes showed the altercation, and that there were no bodies (wounded or dead) on the ground after the prior day's protest had dispersed. As the group debated a crowd of reporters surrounded them. Video cameras covered the verbal confrontation from all angles. A member of the protesters shoved his way through the reporters, emerging a few feet from the Ambassador. When the U.S. representative turned away to answer a question the man from the crowd lunged forward and stabbed the Ambassador below his left shoulder blade. Pandemonium erupted. Marines came out from the Embassy with guns at the ready, as some of them carried the diplomat back inside. The riot police charged into the crowd to push them away from the entrance. Meanwhile, instigators urged the people to stand and fight. Over 100 marchers were injured in the melee. The Ambassador was evacuated to a hospital in Houston. He eventually recovered.

U.S.-Mexican relations, as seen by Bert Maurus, were now on a death watch. In an open break with the Administration the Vice President called reporters into his suite at the Senate Office Building the day after the attack on the Ambassador.

Maurus bluntly condemned Mexico, its Government and its people's "tolerence of evil." He went on to say, "We have seen a most cowardly assault on a brave American, who was defending this nation's honor in the midst of a horde of terrorist sympathizers. As far as I'm concerned the narcotics crime-lords have declared war on the United States of America. The so-called Government of Mexico is obviously incapable of handling the crisis. How many more Americans must pay with their blood for Mr. Stratton's failure to respond as a President must? I had hoped to offer my political experience to Mr. Stratton as he assumed the office of President. He is, as all Americans know, a rookie in the affairs of State. He is use to taking orders, not deciding policy. Before it is too late, I call once again on Cory Stratton to accept my offer of experienced advice. We, as a nation, must deal effectively, decisively and immediately with the criminal conspiracy that is rooted in Mexico."

Never before in American history had a Vice President so publicly challenged the authority of a President. Since he is an elected official the Vice President cannot be dismissed from office by the President. A cold, sharp telephone call from the President's Chief of Staff to Bert Maurus later in the day sternly informed him his presence would no longer be tolerated inside the White House.

Perhaps in any other circumstances Bert Maurus would have issued his political obituary. However, the scenes of an angry mob surrounding a beleaguered Embassy brought to mind the hostage crisis that crippled the Carter Administration. News stories and commentaries in all media forms kept raising this point of reference; and for emphasis, images of the blood-stained Ambassador sprawled on the ground were included with the presentations. Undocumented charges won every foot race with fact as a flood-tide of indignation, and accompanying media frenzy, swept the country.

A trend towards a hyper-reactive media on certain topics had been building in America since the 1980s—when it was not wallowing in the fluff of celebrities or the gore of crime or accidents. The Internet-based Information Age accelerated the process. The web gave birth to a breeding ground of opinion-laced conjecture that became accepted as gospel truth in the click of a mouse by those who considered all traditional information sources as tainted by commercial interests. Initially the Stratton Administration refused to be drawn into the maelstrom. The President strived to avoid any public criticism of the Vice President; he considered such verbal brawling as unseemly for the Presidency. He limited his comments on Maurus' behavior to statements such as: "Administration policy has been settled on the issue. We consider Mexico a vital and reliable ally in our actions against the cartel."

Various spokespersons issued benign statements calling on Americans to use their good judgement in considering the ramifications of the complex issue. Jingoistic rhetoric did not contribute to well-reasoned policy considerations, they said. All of this was lost in the media demand for "red meat" sound bites and video clips. The professional hard-news journalists felt themselves pressued by their corporate management about losing market share if they did not join the swarm which trailed the Vice President at every turn. A few reports began to appear hinting at the possibility that Maurus might challenge Stratton for the nomination in 2012. As the obsession with Mexico entered its second week the Administration sent its senior Cabinet officers to make the rounds of the Sunday morning talk shows. Their appeals for calm, their detailed explanations of Mexico's co-operation, and their assurances that President Stratton was dutifully handling an extremely difficult crisis helped cap some of the concern within the Beltway. However, the country at large was unsure. A Gallup poll found that 47% disapproved of the way Stratton was handling the Mexico issue, 42% approved and 11% were undecided. The question of a more dramatic incursion into Mexican territory was deadlocked at 40%-40%. A slight majority (54%) said it was a good idea for the Vice President to have an independent opinion from the President on this topic. A survey by the Washington Post indicated that a majority of the staff of six of the 14 Cabinet members agreed, at least somewhat, with Bert Maurus' advocacy of "enhanced defensive deployment."

\* \* \* \* \*

Summer thunderstorms are awesome displays of electrical and auditory energy; yet for all the force and fury they are relatively short-lived events. The Mexican crisis by early September seemed to be settling into such a pattern. A return to normalcy was not in the interest of a certain observer. Alex Poller lamented to the Vice President, in a meeting at the Naval Observatory, that he feared a vital opportunity for them was slipping away. Maurus noted in his diary that he was not worried. "You always seem to turn events our way by force of will power," Maurus remarked to Poller.

(Much of what is recounted in this book regarding conversations between Maurus and Poller comes from several notebooks the Vice President maintained during the primaries and his time in office. Remarks were based on tapes from a miniature recorder Maurus carried with him everywhere. The books were sent to this reporter following the events of July 4, 2010.)

In a later entry the Vice President wondered how much jest actually applied to Poller's influence on events.

\* \* \* \* \*

The Durango cartel had once been a loose alliance of five varying-size organizations. At any given time they were as likely to be warring among themselves as engaging in shared enterprises. In the late-90s the largest of these outfits, which was based in the Sierra Madre highlands of central Mexico, experienced a particularly bloody change of leadership. A second-tier divisional organizer, known outside the group even today only as El Guadana, had grown tired of the inflexible methods and routines of the drug traffickers. He wanted to inject a new driving force, a keener business sense, to reach for new horizons, to (frankly) kill anyone who stood in his way of controlling what became a multi-billion dollar enterprise.

By 2004 El Guadana, having murdered and bribed his way to the top of his local group, then employed similar tactics in acquiring control of the country's other major drug-peddling operations. The merger allowed the Durango Cartel (the name is based on El Guadana's favorite movie, the 1971 Western "Arriva Durango, Pago O Muori" [Durango Is Coming, Pay or Die]) to increase its immense income through re-engineered operations. Such lurative results drew the attention of Colombia's drug cartel-dependent Government. The difficulties of the de Valera Administration were a signal to Bogota that Mexico could be ripe for plucking. Beginning in the Spring of 2009 a stream of weapons, communications equipment and advisers began infiltrating Mexico from Colombia, and making its way to the Durango cartel.

El Guadana decided to invest some of the cartel's wealth in the pockets of selected high-ranking Mexican Army officers. Word seeped through the labyrinth of the military that constitutional rule was headed the way of the Aztecs. It would be up to each regional commander to decide his own course of action.

On September 18, 2009 the first major blow was struck in what became the Mexican Civil War. Shortly before dawn an armed force estimated at 5000 men, including elements of the Army, seized control of the city of Hermosillo in the State of Sonora (which borders Arizona and New Mexico). A new Second Republic was proclaimed, and all opponents of the existing order were called upon to join the rebellion. Within days many other municipalities and towns in Sonora were seized or announced their acceptance of the new Republic. This uprising was directed and financed by the cartel.

When President de Valera denounced the rebels and ordered the military to arrest the ring leaders his orders were ignored. Repeated telephone calls and aides sent by de Valera to the Army's General Staff were evasively responded to with remarks indicating the situation was under review. Finally, on the 22nd Army units in the capital took action. However, this action was to set up blockades throughout the city, to barricade de Valera inside the Presidential palace, and to oust all occupants from the buildings used by the members of Congress. The Army Chief of Staff announced that the nation was in a period of grave emergency, and that politicians were unable to cope with the challenge. He described the Second Republic as a farce, and said it would be dealt with shortly.

In reaction, additional Army units in the north joined the Sonora rebellion, and two fronts opened in the south. In Vera Cruz the MPR established their losing candidate in the prior year's election as the "true President" of Mexico; while in Chiapas a long-running Indian uprising flared back to life. By the 30th all six Mexican States bordering the U.S, plus Baja California Sur were controlled by the mixture of cartel and military units which now comprised the Second Republic's defense forces.

President de Valera was offered the choice of seeking asylum in the American Embassy by the Mexican Army's local commander, but he refused. The Army reacted by severing all communication and utility connections to the Palace. Outside contact was maintained by a battery-operated radio transmitter found in one of the offices. The remainder of the nation was experiencing a wide variety of consequences from the discord. Some areas were in complete chaos as competing gangs tried to seize control, while other regions maintained a fragile status quo.

Despite being a silent partner in the Second Republic, the Durango Cartel could not escape its nature as a criminal organization. Its smuggling operations continued, and on October 4th one such caper moved the crisis to the next level of anxiety.

President Stratton had been in constant meetings with members of the National Security Council, Congressional leaders and Pentagon representatives. For all his desire to help Cory Stratton saw little possibility to aid the constitutional Government of Mexico. A highly classified evaluation by the Joint Chiefs of Staff bluntly stated, "Unless the Administration is willing to deploy -at a minimum- a half million American military personnel into the worst kind of guerrilla warfare the United States has no platform from which to unilaterally restore order within Mexico."

\* \* \* \* \*

All the too obvious cliches regarding pending disasters came true in the early hours of October 4th, near the town of Antelope Wells, New Mexico. The cartel expected a confrontation as it set up the smuggling run, and prepared a response. It had previously issued a statement to the media that the Second Republic "was prepared to deal with any challenge to its interests."

When the cartel's convoy detected the advance of a U.S. border patrol it immediately called for back-up forces. As the American troops, three heavily-armed squads of the Army's 7th Cavalry, approached the convoy they were also awaiting assistance. One soldier described the situation, "It got ugly real fast."

The cartel forces initiated action by launching flares over the American position, followed by a mortar attack. Arriving on the scene within minutes were two helicopter gunships manned by renegade Mexican soldiers. These crafts unleashed a barrage of rifle-propelled grenades plus machine gun fire. One squad was devastated as it bore the brunt of the assault. Help for the Americans came in the form of three fighter planes designed to assist low-light ground attacks. The pilots had monitored radio transmissions by both sides on their approach; the cartel's forces neglected to use a secure channel. The cartel's choppers were caught in the fighters' radar, and then wiped out of the sky by air-to-air missiles. In the time it took the American pilots to check the region for additional aerial targets, the smugglers ground forces became engaged in a full-throttle firefight with the soldiers. A call for help brought the planes back; they unloaded missiles and cannon fire onto the smugglers. The entire confrontation lasted less than a half hour. Its impact reached far beyond the tragic scene where eleven Americans died. The cartel's casualties were 18 dead and seven wounded. Twenty-four Mexican civilians were found alive in a trailer.

* * * * *

By 5AM that day President Stratton was in the Oval Office with his major advisers. The Vice President had been reluctantly notified, but did not arrive until 5:20. When Maurus entered the President's face became sterner than it had been and he said, "Maurus, I'm not interested in listening to any nonsense about re-enacting Pershing's raid. The guys at the Pentagon, whom I know and trust far better than I do you, have told me what price we would have to pay in American lives if I went by your 'experienced' advice. If you have something worthwhile to say come in, otherwise you can leave."

"Mr. President. My career has been dedicated to the well-being of this great country. As Vice President I have an obligation to protect America. I will stay and offer what appropriate advice I can. Please continue your discussion."

These words were delivered in tones as icy as the brisk morning air outside the White House. Also in attendance were the Secretaries of Defense and State, the National Security Advisor, the Chairman of the Joint Chiefs, and the President's Chief of Staff. The Congressional leadership was scheduled to meet with Stratton at 6:30.

Bert Maurus endured what he considered five minutes of

futile jaw-flapping. "None of this is getting us anywhere," Maurus finally spat out.

"Excuse me!" shot back the President.

"Mr. Vice President..," the Secretary of State began, but fell quiet with a sharp look from Stratton.

"Maurus, I said..."

"Mr. President! A dramatic move is needed," Maurus rapidly spoke over the President's words. "Mexico is in total chaos, but we can shock it back into order. We can tract the head of the cartel through his cell phone use. Then we can take him out. We can deploy New York's 10th Mountain Division along with the 82nd Airborne, and announce we're acting to defend Mexico's legitimate rulers. De Valera can't object. We'd be saving his neck. Their Army will respond..."

"Their Army will respond," retorted the President, "by attacking our troops as invaders! You can't be that stupid, or are you? Maurus, for the last time—either say something intelligent or get out!"

The tension was palpable to the extent that the two Secret Service Agents in the room moved noticeably closer to the President. Maurus rose slowly. "I am shocked by your cowardice," he said. He turned and left the room, to the audible relief of the Agents. In a hallway nearby Maurus was handed a copy of the Washington Times by his aide, Alex Poller. Beneath the three inch high headline of "Will Cory Act?" was a gory description of the battle at Antelope Wells.

"Has he come to his senses?" Poller asked. Maurus glared at him and stormed out of the building. Poller caught up to the Vice President before he entered his limousine. "Didn't he listen to you?"

Maurus began a reply, then thought better of it with so many witnesses. He whispered, "That damn fool refuses to act. He wants the diplomats to talk—probably until half of the Southwest has been killed by these hoods!"

"But what are you going to do?" Poller demanded. "The

morning talk shows are all a-buzz on what they're calling a growing war fever. The web and satellite radio sites are already gone over the top. Everyone in that flea-speck of a town seems to have been interviewed. And they're all ready to march south today. You have to move on this NOW! We also have to think about the Canadians. The four Premiers are planning next week on calling an assembly of the region's national parliament legislators. They were hoping for support from you on their proposal of opening discussions with this country. But if soldier boy is going to come across as a spineless fool, the whole deal could collapse."

As the Vice President stepped into the car he kept muttering "Let me think, let me think." Poller entered after him. The roadway outside the White House grounds had become a parking lot for media vehicles. Police and the Secret Service took several minutes to clear a path for the limo; when the news crews realized it was Maurus' vehicle a sizable portion abandoned their waiting game to pursue a more likely prospect. On the journey to the Naval Observatory, Maurus channel-surfed across a video world that was foaming at the microphone for action. Antelope Wells had become the new Century's "Maine" cause to be remembered. What came to be seen as the American retreat from/abandonment of Basraistan left a growing sense of bitter frustration in the psyche of many Americans. They felt the need to redeem the nation's honor. Throttling a band of thugs who dared to defy, defile America would set things right.

"What the hell can I do?" Maurus finally asked. "I can't order in the troops. I can't ask Congress for a declaration of war. The only constitutional responsibility I have is to wait around in case the President croaks or is croaked."

"Or fails to carry out his powers and duties," added Poller.

"Yeah, if we were dealing with a President who was medically brain-dead instead of figuratively brain-dead," laughed Maurus.

"It doesn't have to be medical," Poller pointed out. "The Constitution, specifically the 25th Amendment, says nothing about disability." He opened his briefcase, and took out a paperback copy of the document. "Sections 3 and 4 simply state 'unable to discharge the powers and duties.' There's no defination of what that means. Here's the good part. Section 4 provides for the Vice President and a majority of the Cabinet to declare the President 'unable.' If the President fights the designation, then it's up to Congress to referee the question."

Maurus grabbed the book from Poller, read the relevant sections and asked, "How does this help me? What am I suppose to do? This wording is dangerously vague. It's like a loaded gun in a room full of drunks. Besides, what chance would I have?"

Poller looked at him with a cold-blooded smirk. "Yesterday we would have had no chance at all. Today makes a difference. We know a sizable block of the Cabinet is supportive of your call for assertive action. If Stratton doesn't react muscularly it puts pressure on the others to abandon him. Either Stratton does something big immediately, or I'm setting things in motion. Then we'll see how lucky he is this time."

Maurus sat staring ahead, saying nothing. Finally he replied, "It has to be carefully done. It can't look like a putsch. Express it in terms of concern for national security, about the urgent need for decisive leadership. We could do a meeting...an informal one, at the Observatory. None of their aides, just the Secs themselves. Hold off until Stratton makes an announcement. It's got to seem like it's all his fault."

President Stratton did in fact speak to the nation that evening at 9PM, Eastern Time. He expressed the country's anguish over the tragic events, and reiterated his determination to safeguard America's borders. The unravelling conditions in Mexico were presented as an explanation of why unilateral intervention could not succeed. Stratton announced that a conference of the heads of government of the OWHS member States would be held in Washington in two days time. Mexico would be represented by its Ambassador to the U.S. For now, additional Federal troops were being deployed in all four Border States, and naval patrols were being stepped up in the Gulf and along the southern California coastline. The President asked for the prayers and support of all Americans in this extremely difficult time.

Following the speech commentators on all media providers offered their evaluation. On the CBS network Roger Mudd, the anchor of the Evening News for more than a quarter of a century—a triumph of experience over celebrity glitter, remarked, "President Stratton remains an oasis of calm in a city, a nation and a world seemingly determined to shout themselves into a penultimate showdown. For all his military experience, and perhaps because of it, Mr. Stratton has avoided saber-rattling. A rapidly growing number of people in Congress and across America no longer want to 'walk softly.' Increasingly they want the Administration to employ 'the big stick.' Any incursion against Mexico would require an effort far greater than those seen in Cuba, Grenada or Panama. Yet, the President may find a more contentious opposition here at home if he seeks to stay the course of the diplomacy-based policy he set forth tonight."

Alex Poller was on the 'phone with selected Cabinet members less than five minutes after the President concluded his remarks. The members were all cautious in apprasing the speech, however some were willing to offer criticisms under prompting by Poller. By midnight he had arranged a meeting of eight Cabinet members and the Vice President to begin at the Naval Observatory at 9AM. Poller advised the Secretaries to come alone, and not to advise their staff or list the appointment on any of their calendars.

# A Constitutional Coup

Monday, October 5th, 9AM:

ON A WIDE TABLE in the entrance hallway of the Vice President's residence was an array of the day's major newspapers. Each publication devoted its front page to the events at Antelope Wells. Many included sidebar articles summarizing reactions from around the country. The overriding theme was one of concern—concern that a forceful American response could lead to a deeper, treacherous involvement in Mexico's internal crisis—concern that the lack of such a response could lead to something worse.

Post-it notes had been attached to the editorial pages. Some offered conditional support for what was viewed as the President's measured reaction. Many editorials complained about what they described as Stratton's wait and see attitude. The San Diego Observer flatly proclaimed: "Cory Stratton's failure to launch decisive action against repeated invasions of American soil, and the cold-blooded murder of American citizens, renders him unfit to continue as President. He must resign for the good and the safety of the nation." A copy of this editorial was placed before the chair awaiting each Secretary.

The eight Cabinet Secretaries in attendance were: Lewis

Clark—Interior (former Senator from Wyoming), John Holstein—Agriculture (fromer Representative from Iowa), Richard Kresge—Commerce (former Governor of Indiana), Mike Rickles—Labor (former CEO and one-time shop steward of Help-You-Do-It, Inc.), Claire Barton—Health and Human Services (former Representative from California), Zachary Lefrak—Housing and Urban Development (former CEO of Island Homes, Inc.), Lisa Ford—Transportation (former Senator from Michigan), and Frank Benjamin—Energy (former Representative from Texas).

The Cabinet members had entered the grounds of the Naval Observatory through a little-used and little-known back road in order to avoid notice by the hovering media on the main street. Vice President Bert Maurus appeared a few minutes after the visitors had been greeted at the entrance by Alex Poller, and escorted into the conference room. Maurus went around the room to each Secretary, shaking hands and engaging in personal chit chat. With the pleasantries dispensed with, and a supply of coffee and Danish having been delivered, the group sat down with attention riveted on the Vice President.

"I thank you all again for agreeing to come here this morning. This is a difficult time for America. The people are looking to this Government for answers, and so far they haven't been given anything satisfactory. I have personally tried on several occasions to gain the President's acceptance for a forceful response to the drug cartel's murderous attacks. Regretfully, I have not been successful. Perhaps the fault is partially mine. I was, after all, the prime competitor of the President for the nomination last year; and, politics being politics—as you all know—things are said in the heat of battle that professionals agree to overlook once they get down to the business of governing. Mr. Stratton may still hold some of my exuberant commentary against me. I forgave him for what he hurled at me."

"We are professional politicians here," Maurus continued. "Including our two guys from the market place. Mike, Zach...you've helped the Party in fund-raising efforts and as Co-Chairmen of your State organizations. You all know how the game is played. We all understand politics. That's why I worked with the National Committee and recommended each of your appointments to the Cabinet. Politics is part of what we're up against in this Mex mess. If we can't handle it, the voters are going to take their revenge. Our own jobs are safe until '12, but the Congressional elections next year could be a disaster. The other Party hasn't come up with any bright ideas so far. Yet that won't stop them from reminding the people if we drop the ball. Saving this country also means saving our political necks. A policy failure could mean not just some set backs, it could be total annihilation. Remember the Tories in Canada? They went from 200 plus seats to two seats in one election 'cause the voters were annoyed about the economy. We're up against a national security crisis! If our Party is viewed as responsible for appeasement towards narco-terrorists WE ARE GOING TO BE SLAUGHTERED!" (Maurus made this last point as he thumped his fist on the table.)

"Mr. Vice President...OK...Bert...what can we do about it?" asked the Interior Secretary, technically the senior member in attendance. (Seniority is based on the year the Cabinet post was established.) "Stratton is the President. We can offer advice. But it's up to him to do the job."

"Lewis, that's the point I've been trying to avoid. However, there doesn't seem to be any way around it. Stratton isn't doing his job. He's letting things drift, he's letting the American people down, he's in danger of dragging us down with him. He only wants to listen to the Big Four-Defense, State, Treasury and the Attorney General. None of them has political experience. They're all outsiders. Even the other two, Veterans Affairs and Education, are friends of Stratton. Their loyalty is to him. They aren't dedicated to promoting the Party like we are."

"Stratton is getting bad advice from them," said Maurus. "Even so, he should be able to make better decisions. He presented himself to the Party as a man of action. Now he's a symbol of inaction. He doesn't appear to be qualified for the Presidency. We are obligated to the American people to stop this disaster before it gets worse! We must take control of the situation!"

"By taking what course of action?" asked Lisa Ford.

"Under the authority of the 25th Amendment, the Vice President and a majority of the Cabinet can declare that the President is unable to perform his duties, thereby relieving him from office," Maurus flatly stated.

The impact of the words struck the Secretaries like a blow. Every member tried to speak at once, some getting to their feet. No one wanted to believe what they had just heard. Mike Rickles, with plenty of prior experience, managed to outshout the tumult. "Are you out of your damn mind, Maurus? I knew the Constitution provided for a transfer of power, but this is stupidly insane! You can't oust a President simply because you disagree with him. Stratton would have every right to bust in here and arrest us for treason."

Maurus waived everyone to their seat, and sought to assure them. "It's not like that at all, Mike...Alex, hand out those copies...Here's the wording of the Amendment. This is not an ordinary policy question. The safety of the nation is in doubt. If the cartel seizes control of the Mexican Government, it could then totally command the Army. They might form an axis of terror with Colombia. With the money pool they would have do you want to imagine what weapons they could buy on the underground market? Do you know what's still listed as missing from the arsenal of the old People's Republics of Eurasia? We've got to take decisive action before it gets far worse than it is. Stratton won't act. He's not using his powers, he's not fulfilling his duties."

In a quieter voice he continued, "I realize unseating a President is a fateful step. Remember though, we have taken an oath to defend America, her people and her laws. The 25th permits us to set in motion the legal steps necessary to determine the fitness of Cory Stratton to remain as President. A decision by us today is not the final word. Stratton can file his own statement opposing our view; perhaps what we do here today will be shock therapy for him. Maybe he would come to his senses and accept sound advice. If he opposes us the issue must be resolved by Congress. The people's representatives will debate and decide if Stratton is capable of leading America. If we do nothing America doesn't become safer, America remains without an effective response to the narco-terrorists. We will look weak to them, and that invites further acts of war. How many Americans must die before a decision is made to crush our enemies? Stratton refuses to carry out his duties. Are we going to follow the same path of lethal incompetence?"

The Cabinet members were dumbfounded. The implications of either alternative were grimly apparent. "We are truly damned if we do, and damned if we don't," Lewis Clark said in breaking the awkward hush that had fallen over the room. "How much time do we have to decide, Bert?"

"You must do so now," answered the Vice President. Moans escaped from several of the Secretaries. "I know it's difficult. Duty often is difficult. Yet if we delay, word may leak out, the story could get muddled, and it would only deepen the crisis.

Please. I must ask for your decision now; and, it must be unanimous. A majority of the Cabinet must concur. You are that majority. Yes, I wanted to be President; but, I pledge you my solemn vow, this is not a power grab. I love this country as much as you do. I only want what's best serves the people. Let us begin the process. Deciding to do nothing does not solve the crisis. Deciding to do nothing, Stratton's option so far, has made matters worse."

"What do you say?...Lewis? Zach? Lisa? Mike? John? Richard? Claire? Frank?"

They were all fretful, most averted their eyes. "OK," said Maurus. "Let me put it to you bluntly. Each of you owes your appointment to me. I made it happen. Stratton didn't know enough about your level of the bureaucracy to care to find out who belonged where. He handed it over to the National Committee. I found out about the hand-off. You were all on my A-list. You're my people. Now it's time for pay back. Even if I lose this gamble you don't want to be on my bad side if you want a future in this Party. I want your verbal and written affirmation of support for this undertaking—now. Alex, hand out the statement for them to sign. Well, boys and girls, what's it going to be?"

"Why cant' we go to the President as a group and explain our concerns?" asked Claire Barton. "He's been so wrapped up in this problem, he hasn't had time to call a full Cabinet meeting. If we present a united front, voice our anxieties, surely the President will listen."

Bert Maurus glared across the table at her. "The very fact," he countered, "that he hasn't met with you is prime evidence he doesn't care what you think. He held a dawn confab with his inner circle yesterday. Did he call any of you? Stratton has walled himself off. He doesn't want to hear troubling alternate opinions. It's as if he waiting for someone to tell him what to do, but he won't heed anyone since he outranks everyone. Think for a moment! Here we are, a roomful of some of this country's major officials. A titanic crisis grips our society. Has anyone from the White House beeped anyone here, asking them to urgently come today to 1600? Or at any time since the last full Cabinet meeting—in JULY? No competent President would commit, or tolerate, such an error. Voters will have the right to ask what we did to handle this mess. Do you want to go before the American people and say 'I couldn't act because Cory wouldn't give me permission.'"

Bert Maurus had honed his talent of effectively delivering speeches during more than thirty years in politicking. He also made it a point of knowing his audience beforehand. He came prepared to tell the Cabinet members what he needed them to hear. Maurus was keenly aware of the background of each person in the room. They were intelligent, well-meaning, dedicated folks who were amazed at their good fortune. At best they were good second-class professionals whose advancements had depended on party loyalty. Here now was the man who had brought them to the zenith of their careers saying they were obligated to support his proposal to overthrow the President of the United States.

Maurus also played to their vanity. They were notable figures in the Government, their nominations had been confirmed by the Senate (with favorable airtime on C-SPAN and their local TV network), reporters (occasionally) sought their opinion, they were VIPs in their home towns. How would it play on Main Street if the local paper stated they had done nothing about Mexico, had not spoken out, that their views were not even sought by the President? Fearful of acting, but dreading irrelevance, each Secretary reluctantly picked up the pen laid out, and signed the challenge to Cory Stratton's continued service as President. Alex Poller went around the table collecting the documents.

Do you agree with my proposal?" asked Maurus as he pointed at them one by one. In a strained voice or harsh whisper each answered "yes."

* * * * *

## Monday, October 5th, 1pm:

The contents of the simultaneously delivered packages to President Cory Stratton, Speaker of the House Todd Poorberry of California, and President Pro Tempore of the Senate Monty Thorstrom of Delaware created a level of stunned bewilderment not seen since the 1981 videotape showing then President Michael Morrison (an Offensive Linesman on his college football team) pummeling a would-be assassin to the ground after the gunman's weapon misfired at point-blank range.

The packages, which were large envelopes bearing the official seal of the Vice President, contained copies of the documents signed by the eight Cabinet Secretaries and the Vice President. Attached was a cover letter signed by Bert Maurus invoking the terms of Section 4 of the 25th Amendment. The letter in part declared: "Whereas it is the considered judgment of the Vice President and a majority of the Cabinet that Cory Stratton has demonstrated an unwillingness to fully discharge his power to defend the United States in regards to the Mexican emergency, such unwillingness is in the considered judgment of the Vice President and a majority of the Cabinet sufficient proof that Cory Stratton is unable to perform his duty as President to defend the United States. The limited response undertaken by Cory Stratton in reaction to the invasion of American territory by hostile foreign nationals, and the murder of American citizens by these hostile foreign nationals, has severely compromised the security of America and her citizens. As a result of the attached declaration signed by the Vice President and a majority of the Cabinet, we deem Cory Stratton removed from the office of President of the United States, and that Vice President Bertford Maurus has now assumed that office as Acting President."

The two Congressional leaders immediately telephoned the White House after reviewing the contents of the package. They were almost as immediately on their way to the Oval Office for a conference with President Stratton, his Chief of Staff, the Senior White House Counsel, Attorney General Billie Fallwigs, and the Secretaries of State, Defense and Treasury. All agreed to issue no comment unless Maurus went public with his demand. Stratton expressed a hope that Maurus was engaged in a bluff, and would back down if he were ignored. The hope died soon thereafter. At 5PM messengers from the Vice President arrived at the Washington headquarters of the five broadcast networks and of World Network News, the leading cable news network, delivering to each a package for the executive in charge of the news division. This time Maurus included a video tape of himself reading the cover letter. Standing in the background was a morose-looking group of eight Cabinet Secretaries. A flood of 'phone calls rumbled across the capital's fiber-optic lines to the White House, the Congressional leaders and the Naval Observatory. By 5:30 all the networks were on the air with the most startling political story of the new (and perhaps even the prior) Century. The radio and web affiliates of the TV networks were the next source to announce details on the astonishing maneuver by the Vice President. Independent television and radio stations quickly joined in, and chat rooms on the Internet expanded at a seemingly speed of sound rate.

The general public, to put in mildly, was thunderstruck. Outside the Beltway the actions and views of most Vice Presidents receives little attention from the American populace. Maurus was no exception. His fifteen minutes of fame occurred during the primaries, but once the nomination was beyond his grasp he faded from the headlines. Although Maurus had made provocative statements on the Mexico crisis, he remained in the background of most peoples' awareness of events; his public outbursts against the President were one-day wonders in the news for them. People considered his remarks part of the normal nonsense that is politics. Nothing had prepared them for a Constitutional showdown. That now changed. Residents of large cities bore witness to a scene many believed was extinct: evening editions of major newspapers being sold on street corners with the word EXTRA emblazoned across the front page.

The President's official reaction was the drafting and delivering of a letter to the Speaker and Senate President refuting Bert Maurus' assertions. A copy was sent to the Observatory addressed to Mr. B. Maurus. The Vice

President, observing the Constitutional script, re-sent to the appropriate individuals another copy of his original letter. This one had been re-signed and re-dated by Maurus and the eight Cabinet Secretaries, with the time noted as 8PM. By that hour a literal army of news crews had descended on the Vice President's residence. Network executives in New York and California were conducting desperate searches to charter, rent or purchase any aircraft capable of hauling additional crews and equipment from around the country to Washington, D.C. The United States Air Force turned down several frenzied requests for use of its C-5 Galaxy transport aircraft.

At 9PM President Stratton publicly replied to Maurus' challenge in a globally-televised speech that was also simulcast on the Internet. "Good evening to everyone. I will begin by stating emphatically—I, Cory Stratton, am the President of the United States. I was duly elected by the American voters, and I will complete my full term, so help me God. I have faithfully executed the powers and duties of this office. I am more than capable of continuing to uphold my obligations to the people and the Constitution. I rebut the challenge to my authority. I am prepared to defend my performance and my honor. The policy my Administration is following concerning Mexico has been formulated in wide-ranging thoughtful considerations. My opponents would have us adopt a radical about-face, and proceed on a path that would gravely endanger this country. Their policy is fatally short-sighted. Their views have been raised in the discussions that took place within the Administration. Repeatedly I have found their views to be of doubtful value, with a strong likelihood of pulling this nation into a bloody quagmire. Following consultations with my loyal advisers, and the Congressional leadership, I will go to Capitol Hill on Thursday to defend this Administration before Congress. A special joint session will be held for this purpose, and to provide time for any presentation by my challengers. I have been in hard fights before, and I have won. I will win this one as well. God bless you. God bless the United States of America."

\* \* \* \* \*

TUESDAY AND WEDNESDAY, OCTOBER 6TH AND 7TH:

The opening rounds of baseball's post-season play, the NFL's regularly scheduled games and the start of a major golf tournament all took place this week. People went about their usual activities. It was possible to escape the agitated point-counter point confrontations being offered by the multitude of information-providing services. Survey takers were frustrated in their initial efforts to monitor America's pulse because so many people either hung up or launched into free-fire monologues on the issue of the day. Finally, by late Wednesday a picture began to emerge of a nation prepared for a drastic decision, but uncertain of what it wanted that decision to be. Overall 45% thought Cory Stratton was doing a fair to good job, 42% said he was performing badly, and 13% were unsure. When questioned further of those who said Stratton was performing badly a significant number (33% of this group) said their position was influenced by the presentation of accusations in the media.

Yet the survey also found that 60% of those replying would support the President if he ordered an invasion of Mexico to wipe out the cartel. (A military option was favored by 80% of those in the front-line States of California, Arizona, New Mexico, Texas and Florida.) An almost equal number believed that a state of war already existed with Mexico. 4% said they would not object to the use of "tactical or limited range" nuclear weapons against the cartel's headquarters region.

43% said Stratton should be forced to resign, or be impeached, if he failed to attack Mexico in the event of another raid by any armed force from Mexico. 36% opposed this idea. 21% were undecided.

72% knew the Constitution had some type of provision for transferring power if a President died or became severely ill. 99% were clueless about the details of Section 4 of the 25th Amendment.

64% said they did not know enough about Bert Maurus to judge his actions. 20% favored the holding of an election to let the people choose between Stratton and Maurus. 7% of those interviewed did not know, prior to Monday's events, that Bert Maurus was the Vice President.

\* \* \* \* \*

A more ominous reading of opinion was being provided to the President. His own chief pollster advised Stratton that a sizable number in Congress were prepared to endorse Bert Maurus' application of "25/4" (the short-hand term which evolved to indicate the relevant Constitutional provision); Members of the House and Senate from the front-line States were concerned about the upcoming elections and wanted somebody to fix the problem fast. Adding to the President's difficulties was the stance taken by House Speaker Todd Poorberry. The Speaker's own district was in Orange County of southern California. His constituents were among the more vociferous proponents of a demand for military action. The Speaker had announced on Wednesday that the House vote on 25/4 would be a free vote—no persuasion would be applied, one way or the other, by the party's whips.

By agreement with the Senate President, Poorberry released a statement Wednesday evening with the schedule of activities. The House and Senate would meet in joint session on Thursday (the 8th) to hear the President speak; the Vice President would speak on Friday (the 9th). Both would be available to answer questions later in the day from Members of Congress, but not from the news media or the public. Unless additional time was requested, the House would debate the issue on Saturday (the 10th) and vote on Monday (the 12th).

If the House supported Maurus on 25/4, then the Senate

would debate it on Tuesday (the 13th). In order for Maurus' challenge to be successful he had to obtain a 2/3 majority or better in each chamber. If not the challenge could not be re-submitted unless it was on a premise other than "unwillingness equals unable." Therefore, to get past the first hurdle Bert Maurus needed the votes of at least 294 of the 441 Members of the House of Representatives.

The President's pollster found on Wednesday near unanimous support for 25/4 among the House delegations from California, Arizona, New Mexico, Texas and Florida. The remaining House Members were nearly evenly divided between "yes," "no" and "undecided." The Senate was also split into three factions—40 would vote "yes" to support Maurus, 32 would vote "no" and 30 were undecided.

\* \* \* \* \*

## Thursday, October 8th:

Congress will often labor long and hard in its efforts to deal with major issues. Yet it will also insist on its sessions beginning at a reasonable (often post-lunch) hour. The assembling of the people's legislature to consider this most unique Constitutional question was slated to begin at the unusual hour of 9AM. This meant that Representatives, Senators, their staffs, the news media, members of the President's and Vice President's staffs, and the general public began arriving on Capitol Hill before 6AM.

Along Pennsylvania Avenue, from the White House to Capitol Hill, crowds had been gathering since the prior evening. President Stratton's motorcade would take this route sometime after 8:30. Few of those waiting along the sidewalk would actually see Stratton. His car would whiz by in seconds, and it was unlikely that the President would be waving from the window. A blustery northeast wind and low cloud deck further discounted such behavior. Yet moments of history draw people. They want to say later that they personally witnessed some part of it live, not filtered through the unblinking eye of television. They want to experience the tension, or the electricity, or the dourness of the moment. Conspiracy—legal and in full view—is as compelling a drama as the after-effects of unexpected tragedy. The crowds on this day were said to be the largest since the 1933 funeral for the assassinated President-elect Franklin Roosevelt.

[This tragic event occurred in Miami on February 15, 1933. It produced a Constitutional crisis of its own. There was no provision in the Constitution for replacing a President-elect. A bi-partisan conference of major political leaders devised a solution. Vice President-elect John Gardner was sworn in as scheduled on Inauguration Day (March 4th). The Chief Justice then publicly stated that the office of the President was vacant, and swore in Gardner as President.]

Through this array of human expectations President Cory Stratton proceeded on the most agonizing morning of his brief political career. Accompanying Stratton was his wife, Elizabeth. She had often expressed her private fears to him about the brutal potential of American politics. Never in her worst nightmare had she foreseen such a horror as now confronted her husband.

They seemed an odd match, poster people for an opposites attract campaign. Elizabeth Chisholm Stratton, five years younger and a foot shorter, had first seen Cory Stratton while both were stationed at a NATO base in the then West Germany nearly 30 years ago.

[Germany was re-united after the collapse of the PREA.]

Elizabeth was a trauma surgeon at the base hospital, and they were introduced to each other by a mutual friend. Her quiet, reserved nature was a notable contrast to Stratton's usual cohort of demonstrative friends and family. Initially he was uncertain, then delighted by her habit of stopping him in mid-bombastic oratory by smiling and rolling her eyes up. They were married within a year, and by their fifth anniversary were the proud parents of three fine children—

Kenneth, Leo and Tamara. The family endured the nomadic aspect of Cory's military life; finally settling into a permanent home (at least for mother and children) once the offspring reached school age. She had insisted on it.

Elizabeth Stratton chose to remain in the background attending to her patients and children, although Cory's promotion to General often required her to become involved in the military's social circles. She resisted as much as possible. Her forays into public action were usually directed towards fund-raising or volunteer efforts of local hospitals.

As First Lady, Elizabeth Stratton championed the causes of pre-natal, pediatric and pre-school health care programs. During interviews she admitted discussing political matters with her husband, the President. She did not believe this gave her any undue influence over government policy. "If you ever heard some of our discussions," she said, "you would be amazed that we ever agreed on names for our children, never mind budget allocations to subsidize inter-State bus travel in the Corn Belt."

\* \* \* \* \*

She sat beside him now in the Presidential limousine heading southeast along Pennsylvania Avenue, as worn and worried looking as when one of her children had been seriously ill. A shiver ran through her, despite the vehicle's defenses against drafts and other invasive elements.

"Are you cold, Lizzy?" Cory asked.

"What's the saying about sudden chills?" Elizabeth replied. "Something about a person in the future walking over your grave?" She smiled in saying this, but Cory looked grimmer than before. He took her hands and rubbed them softly.

"Don't worry. It'll all be over soon enough, for better or worse. If it turns out poorly we can go away and live in peace. The world can then go spinning off to whatever act of damnation it wants. I won't be responsible for any of it. Perhaps I won't care. If I could dump this job off to someone other than that brazen fool Maurus I'd save Congress the bother, and resign my commission...oops, office. They elect Presidents to perform miracles, then lambast them for failure to be miraculous."

Elizabeth laughed, "You would never give them the satisfaction of seeing you quit. Leathernecks never die even when they're dead. It's the Barbary pirates all over again."

Now it was Cory's time to laugh. "If you try signing the Corps' anthem I'll stop the car and leave you sitting in the middle of the Avenue...Thanks for being here, Lizzy. I know this day is harder for you than it is for me. I'm glad there's one human being nearby who's not trying to push or pull me to suit their sense of historical direction. I'll fight them just to prove you're not married to an addled-brain grunt."

They leaned towards one another, holding hands as the motorcade neared the Capitol. A forest of satellite dishes for the news crews stretched around the building. The Secret Service Agents in position directed the vehicles to a secure side entrance.

A joint session of Congress is always a dramatic affair. It is called on the occasion of a grand political episode, or a heart-rending time of sorrow. As with some in the past, the present one was a mixture. Unlike those in the past, there were significant differences. The Vice President and his eight Cabinet supporters were not in attendance, neither were the Justices of the Supreme Court or the diplomatic corps. Chief Justice Sandra Day O'Connor had decided to absent the Court based on the possibility that the Constitutional confrontation could end up before the nine Justices. The diplomatic corps was usually invited to this State function; but they understood why the pleasure of their company was not requested. The gallery was filled to standing-room only with the family and staff members of the legislators.

As 9AM was announced throughout the city with the ringing of church bells, the Doorkeeper of the House of Representatives stepped forward into the center aisle and declared in a ringing voice: "Mr. Speaker! The President of the United States!"

The doors leading from the outside hallway opened, and Cory Stratton entered. Upon almost any other occasion this would be a cue for a tumultuous greeting from the assembled lawmakers. Those seated along the aisle would reach out for a Presidential handshake, calling his name and words of greeting. Today there were only whispers. The absence of noise was startling. Lasting only seconds, it seemed an eternity. Suddenly a voice, high up and soft, called out "Cory!." The President looked to his right, as the head of the Secret Service detail Agent Ed Seehohen, caught Stratton's elbow and pointed. Above the assembly, in singular assertiveness, Elizabeth Stratton was standing and waving. When the President saw her, he waved back. She then began applauding. The tiny, rhythmic sound was amplified by the chamber's stillness; it shocked the audience into a response. Slowly, fitfully, others stood and applauded. The number grew. Islands of individuals were linked as additional Members were swept into the moment. A few cheers arose. Finally, most (but not all) in the chamber were on their feet, many (but not all) clapping their hands as tradition regained control.

Cory Stratton shook the few outstretched hands near him, and turned once more to wave to Elizabeth. He mouthed a "Thank you. I love you," and blew her a kiss. While the applause lasted, the President made his way to the podium. Seated behind him, on the raised step, were the Speaker and the Senate President. Stratton shook hands with them, and the Speaker graveled for order. The crowd fell silent. Todd Poorberry declared, "Never before in the history of this great Republic have Members of Congress gathered for such an event. The decision we will make in this regard will have a profound affect on the future of America. God help us all! Ladies and Gentlemen of the Congress, the President of the United States."

Applause began around the floor without any prompting by the First Lady. She stood again, waved again, and was the last to be seated.

For a moment the President did not speak. He looked at his notes, folded the sheets and put them away. His words would be his own, rather than the crafted phrases of the White House speech writers.

"Cowardice, in my previous line of work, was a charge subject to a court-martial review board. If the defendant was judged guilty in time of war, the penalty could be death by firing squad. If I cannot persuade you today, I will at least be glad the same penalty does not apply to my current job."

*(A smattering of laughter ran across the assembled group.)*

"I have looked into the eyes of Death on the battlefield, and I did not falter in defense of this great nation. I had the honor of directing other campaigns from headquarters, knowing my decisions were a matter of life and death for many. Again, I did not falter in defense of America. I have seen, held and smelt more dead and dying people than probably most of you in this room. I have commanded everything from a squad to an international coalition of armies. Yes, I have been afraid. No intelligent person in a war scenario could be other than afraid. My training prepared me for such crisis. I know how to make decisions, the right ones for the right time."

"Experience in war is not something a person would choose to obtain. As citizens of a country which desires to remain free, we must undertake certain courses of action we might otherwise wish to defer, in order to defend that freedom. Experience in war teaches those who are fortunate enough, and skillful enough, to survive that winning battles takes more than waving a sword and yelling 'charge!.'"

"Being in the front wave of a stampede is not a position of leadership."

*(Applause from spots around the chamber.)*

"The United States has over one million military personnel, and enough hardware, aircraft and naval vessels to handle several opponents the size and strength of Mexico in a conventional conflict. If I decided as Commander-in-Chief to obliterate the northern portion of Mexico with a torrent of conventional stand-off capacity weapons in order to 'resolve' the cartel problem, such an assault would clearly end up with us being the 'winner'.

"'Oh, no!' you might say, 'that would be too drastic. Find another way.'"

"Perhaps I could send in ground forces—a quarter of a million, a half million—and let them hammer their way south in search of an enemy indistinguishable from the civilian population. There would be considerable 'collateral damage'; however, eventually, two years, five years, who knows, we could declare victory and withdraw. The inhabitants of Mexico, good and evil alike, would have been taught a lesson."

"'Oh, no!' you might say again, 'that would be too dreadful also. Find another way.'"

"One of my predecessors is said to have remarked that the first important lesson you learn about the Presidency is how much you cannot do. I, or any other President, have the Constitutional responsibility to make decisions. What a President understands is that decision-making on vitally critical issues can often be a choice between horrible and disdainful options."

"There is no easy, one-advance-fixes-all decision I can make regarding Mexico. Doing nothing costs lives, intervening militarily would cost lives, anything in between would cost lives. And none of these options can guarantee success for the long-term."

"I am painfully aware of the tragedy that has struck our border region. I want to end the threat posed by the cartel so that it can never again afflict this nation's citizens. The best way to accomplish that goal is to aid the legitimate forces of democracy in Mexico to regain control of the government, so that the government can regain control of Mexico. The law-abiding citizens of Mexico are also suffering in this crisis. Our response must not be such that these citizens are victimized again. I had planned to meet with the heads of Government of the OWHS nations. I would propose a multi-national force be sent to Mexico to restore President de Valera to power. America would be a major contributor to this force in terms of personnel and material. I also planned to announce the Federalization of the National Guard in the four front-line States, and the dispatch of 10,000 Marines to the border area. These matters are not on hold. The Secretary of State will meet today with the OWHS leaders, and the Marines are already on the way."

*(A strong round of applause from many sections of those assembled.)*

"We are an extraordinary civilization. America, unlike other dominant powers in the history of the world, chooses not to bulldoze her way through the course of events. We often seem to have greater feelings for people in other lands than the residents of such countries have for each other or their neighbors. Everyone here can trace their family's roots to a starting point somewhere else on the planet. As the song says, 'We are the world'. No nation wants us involved in their internal affairs until they start yelling at us for ignoring them. We cannot solve every problem. We can do our best in helping to ameliorate those conditions where our participation can make a helpful difference."

"You know who I am. I am a plain-spoken man who will tell you directly what I want to do. You know that I am thoughtful and deliberate, as anyone who has directed the military resources of America needs to be. You know that I am not a coward. You know that I am more than capable of conducting the powers and duties of the Presidency. In a time of crisis, this nation needs calm, effective, resourceful, intelligent, proven leadership. You know that I am the man for this job."

"In this endeavor I need your help. The Constitution has bestowed upon the Members of Congress the responsibility of deciding conflicts of Executive authority. America can have only one President at a time. America needs a leader who can be President, not just act as President. You know that I am the man for this job! Help me help America! God bless you all! God bless the United States of America!"

\* \* \* \* \*

Perhaps without thinking, perhaps by pure emotional response to a dynamically delivered appeal, perhaps without reflection on how they would vote, at least a 2/3 majority of the House and Senate were on their feet loudly applauding Cory Stratton.

Still at the podium, Cory Stratton looked up at his wife and waved. Elizabeth Stratton replied by snapping off a salute crisper than any DI on Parris Island.

\* \* \* \* \*

The speech had been transmitted to the nation and the world. Tens of millions of people witnessed the drama, reactions varying according to their hopes and fears. Several miles from the Capitol two men sat in the study of the Naval Observatory, their hopes turning to fear.

"Damn him to hell!" muttered Bert Maurus. "Doesn't he understand how much trouble he's in? Does he expect anyone to believe that wasn't intensely rehearsed? No one is that good extemporaneously. He can't get away with it… can he? We have to re-write my remarks. First, he can't do anything; now he thinks he's Michael Morrison, the Great Communicator. It took us three days to work up what we have. How can we re-do it by tomorrow morning?"

Alex Poller stood and walked to a window. After a moment, he said, "We can get started in about twenty minutes. You should relax, Mr. Soon To Be President. It isn't practical in these circumstances to lock yourself into a set schedule.

Evolving eras breed instability. Get something from the bar. Let me do some preliminary work before we sketch out refinements in the text. Don't worry. History will judge us fairly in the long run."

\* \* \* \* \*

### Friday, October 9th:

Enrique Cardinale Don Francisco routinely started his day at 4AM since arriving in Washington as Mexico's envoy. Besides the more mundane functions of his position, Cardinale was also responsible for being his Government's life-line to the outside world. He had finally convinced the American President that a multi-national rescue force would be accepted by the Mexican people, provided its sole purpose was the restoration of the de Valera Administration. Yesterday's initial session with the OWHS heads of government had gone well. The Ambassador believed they would endorse President Stratton's call for collective action. The President's speech certainly aided the cause. Today's session would be critical.

Normally, Cardinale departed his Georgetown residence by 6 o'clock. The series of telephone calls he had to make this morning delayed Cardinale. It was nearly 8 before he was prepared to leave. Actually, this was alright. The traffic would be somewhat lighter along his intended route, since his neighbors were dedicated go-getters who would already be at work. Cardinale drove his own car, in keeping with de Valera's policy of a less regal government.

The street outside his home was still. There were no vehicles moving, and only two vans parked along the roadway. Cardinale stepped out through the front doorway, calling back over his shoulder a farewell to his wife. She thought he called out again, but the sound was strange. She did not hear the car being started, so she went to the door...then collapsed to the floor, calling his name.

Within half an hour the news shook the city and country. A typical breaking-news bulletin went as follows: "This just in. Washington, D.C. police and the FBI are investigating the shooting death of Mexico's Ambassador to the U.S.; the Ambassador was gunned down by an unknown assassin as he left his Georgetown home this morning. A police officer with knowledge of the investigation, who spoke on condition of anonymity, said the police have no witnesses or suspects. The single shot, which struck the diplomat in the chest, is believed to have been fired from a high-powered rifle. As you may be aware, Mexico is embroiled in a civil war pitting the Government against the Durango drug cartel and an insurgency of dissident army and political factions. The officer stated it was too early to rule out any possibility; however, the murder in Georgetown could be the latest tragedy in Mexico's turmoil."

\* \* \* \* \*

Saturday October 10th:

The joint session of Congress scheduled for Friday was postponed as reports of the assassination reached Capitol Hill. A measure of heightened anxiety was added to the prevailing somber mood of Washington as nature capped the scene with a slate-gray overcast and a bitter east wind.

Vice President Bert Maurus stood before the gathering of lawmakers shortly before 10AM. Little had changed in the makeup of the audience, save the absence of the President and his Cabinet supporters. The eight Secretaries who endorsed Maurus' invoking of 25/4 were seated in a front row.

Maurus had not requested permission for a grand entrance down the center aisle. The House chamber, where the joint sessions are held, did not have any rules for an address by a Vice President. A new provision would have to be proposed, studied by a committee and finally voted on by the Representatives; Maurus did not have time for such a delay.

Instead, he chose to make a simple but dignified entrance from a side door.

The Speaker introduced him in a straightforward manner. "Ladies and Gentlemen of the Congress, the Vice President of the United States." A mild wave of applause rippled across the chamber. The Members had come to listen, not to declare their intentions just yet. Maurus went to the heart of the issue immediately. "The evil that is destroying Mexican society has now dared to strike at the soul of America. Timid policies do not deter lawlessness. Caution is seen by criminals as evidence of weakness. Swift, strong crackdowns emphatically alert thugs to the danger of assailing a people who respect and defend the rule of law."

"An assassin stalks the streets of this city. A murderer has defiled America's capital. Evil has come to confront those who lacked the courage and foresight to confront it head-on when it first raised itself out of the sewers of hell."

"I have spoken out from the very beginning concerning the critical need to eradicate this terror. My warnings were ignored. Another brave man now lies dead. His name must be listed beside those Americans who have also fallen victim to the violence consuming our southern neighbor. If we do nothing about these murders, we mock the victims and dishonor ourselves. If we continue the ineffective measures offered by Cory Stratton, we will be further shamed."

"America has been violated three times by the terrorists of the Durango drug cartel in military-style assaults. These criminals have killed Americans in cold-blooded defiance of what they perceive as a timid, confused society. The inadequate reaction to the first outrage directly contributed to the occurrence of the other atrocities. Our Ambassador was almost killed. When do we stop wringing our hands, stop whining in fear, and take arms against this sea of terror?"

"We are at war! As surely as if a foreign nation, suddenly and without warning, attacked and destroyed a United States military base. We are at war!"

"The enemy may not parade about in fine uniforms. The enemy may not march as a conventional army. Yet that enemy exists! That enemy has assassinated American citizens. So far the White House seems to have fired off more press releases than our troops have fired off bullets. If a fatally flawed response to aggression is not treason, at least it must be considered incompetence of the worst order."

"We have a man you know in the Oval Office who acknowledges the self-evident gravity of the Mexican crisis, who listens to a small clique of puppets for advice, and who is unable or unwilling to act decisively."

"Our country is in grave danger. We cannot as the responsible members of the Government allow this mortal threat to continue. Cory Stratton is a fine speech-maker; but, he is not responsibly discharging the powers and duties of the Presidency. Cory Stratton has failed to perform his Constitutional obligations. Cory Stratton is unfit to serve as President."

"He has been given advice by myself and the majority of the Cabinet on the urgent need for a different Mexican policy. He has failed to heed that advice."

"He has called upon foreign regimes for permission to undertake a limited-goal operation that does not guarantee the safety of Americans. He has failed to exterminate the citadel of the enemy's network—a site known to the Pentagon, the OSS, the National Reconnaissance Office and the news media."

"Cory Stratton has failed as President. His words on Thursday did not offer any hope for improvement. He made a plea to be allowed to do more of the same, more of the same failures that have led to the deaths of Americans."

"We were elected by the American voters to defend this country, her people, her laws. If we allow Cory Stratton's failed Presidency to continue, we will also be judged as incompetent."

"I ask for your support in upholding the Constitution-based call, by a majority of the Cabinet and myself, that

Cory Stratton be removed from office for his failure to carry out the powers and duties of the Presidency."

"Your duty under the Constitution is clear! Your duty to the American people is clear! You must vote to remove Cory Stratton! You must vote to protect America!"

Bert Maurus had not been interrupted a single time by applause, shouts of approval or opposition. The Members had listened in cold, intense attention. As he completed his oration, Maurus departed the chamber uncertain if he had failed or succeeded.

\* \* \* \* \*

## Monday, October 12th and Tuesday, October 13th:

The House of Representatives assembled for these two days under intense scrutiny and extraordinary pressure. The gallery had been given over to the news media, and virtually every information outlet on the planet had a delegate in attendance. On the floor, each Member was allotted three minutes to state their view on 25/4; this required more than 22 hours of debate, which was spread over the two-day period. One Member was in hospital when the debate began; the Speaker arranged for a telephone link which allowed the Member to announce his opinion from the comfort of his hospital bed. He had an ambulance standing by to deliver him to the House chamber when the vote would be held on Thursday the 15th.

The opinions expressed by the Members keenly reflected the agitated and conflicting views of the American people. The offices of the Representatives were bombarded by telephone calls, e-mail, faxes and yes, even telegrams. On day two of the debate the public's admonishments were reduced to a simple "YES" (in favor of removing Cory Stratton) or "NO" (in opposition to his removal.) As in the House national opinion polls, perhaps influenced by the Mexican Ambassador's murder, showed a plurality of Americans saying "YES." Head counts in the House showed the "Yes" total still short of a 2/3 majority. No new ground was broken in the debate. The arguments and pleas which had rebounded across the chamber for months were again presented. Tempers and voices flared. Ominous predictions by supporters of either view point were made and derided.

By Tuesday night all but four of the lawmakers had declared their intention. The fate of the proposal depended on these Members; for the measure to pass it would require a "Yes" vote from all four. One belonged to the opposition party, the others were veteran Representatives of the President's party. Two were from the West (neither from a Border State), one from the Mid West, and one from the Northeast. They met with Speaker Poorberry at 1AM Wednesday morning in his office. They promised to have a decision by Thursday's session. Making use of decoys and Capitol Hill security guards, the Speaker aided the four Members in eluding the hunting packs of the news media waiting to pounce on them. He had obtained the use of four suites at the Whitewater apartment complex. Each Member could lock themselves in a well-stocked suite until Thursday morning. They each needed time to think separately, and Poorberry (despite his own set view) understood their need for private reflection.

Thursday's session would open at 10AM; the four would each have three minutes to speak. While any one of them was at the podium, the others who had not spoken would be kept off the floor of the House so that there would be no undue last minute influence. They had drawn numbered cards in the Speaker's office on Wednesday morning, indicating their order of addressing the House. The final spot went to Representative Sean Deise of New Jersey's Staten Island/Bayonne district. When he saw the number 4 on the card he selected Deise said he felt as if he had been whacked in the forehead with the

Speaker's gavel. This pang of anxiety was insightful. The deciding vote in the drama would be his.

*****

Thursday, October 15th, 12:07 am

The sound roused him from the sitting room couch. Sean Deise had drifted off into a fitful sleep, and the sudden noise jarred him awake. He realized after a moment that the sound was not an alarm clock, but rather the door chimes of the apartment in the Whitewater complex. He stood and padded to the door in his bare feet. Sean began to undo the locks, however he hesitated on second thought. He glanced through the peep hole and was surprised by who he saw. Standing in the hallway was Alex Poller. "What does he want?" the Congressman muttered to himself.

The chimes rang again, stirring Deise out of his delay. Disengaging the final lock, he pulled open the double doors, and greeted the Vice President's Chief of Staff with a blunt "How the hell did you find me?"

Poller laughed. "You should know by now that very little stays secret for very long in this town." When Deise made no sign of inviting him inside, Poller added "Do you want to discuss this where the neighbors can hear us?"

Deise withdrew a few steps, closing the doors but not locking them once Poller entered. "Did the Speaker send you?"

"No," replied Poller. "Todd wasn't in a sharing mood, so I tapped into alternate sources for information." Waving at the surroundings he added, "This is all very melodramatic if you ask me."

The Congressman walked back to the couch and sat down without inviting Poller to make himself comfortable. Poller followed on his own, choosing a chair not in the line of sight of the windows. "I'm not going to engage you in a debate, Poller. The purpose in coming here was to escape outside influences," said Deise.

Poller leaned forward in his seat, smirking. "Save your speeches for the House. I'm here to talk about reality. Forget about the Constitutional hogwash. This is a bare-knuckle brawl for power. Stratton doesn't know how to use it. Maurus can be trained. We're stuck with dysfunctional yahoos on our borders who are going nova, and threatening to incinerate us in the process. If someone doesn't take command we're going to have bigger difficulties than deciding which prima donna gets to play Big Daddy to all us small fries."

"I'm offering you the chance to be a major player. You can have a blank check that you can cash in anytime, if you vote the right way. Of course, the only restriction is that you can't be President. Not right away, that is. If you're interested in that job we can build you up. You're a young guy, so there's plenty of time. A Senate seat would be a good warm-up. Do the right thing, make the right people happy…we know how to reward our friends. In the meantime, maybe there's other things you need. We can work it out. Reasonable people can easily come to a satisfactory arrangement. Whataya say?"

The Congressman shook his head. "Do you think this is just another omnibus appropriations bill we're marking up? Do for me and I'll do for you. I'm only in my third term but I'm not stupid or a novice. I worked in Trenton before coming down here. Wheeling and dealing is part of the game. If citizens knew what we did in conference meetings to work out legislative compromises, they'd have our heads. That doesn't mean everything has to be reduced to a trade-off item. Some of us still believe in principles!"

"Grow a brain!" barked Poller. "You're not Jimmy Stewart and this isn't a scene from 'Mr. Smith Goes to Washington.' Get real. Are you going to throw away your future because the civics text books say you should be a starry-eyed boy wonder? Hell, they don't even teach civics in most schools any more. Listen, I can get Maurus to initiate policies, once he's President, that will expand the size and influence of the United States. We were meant to control this continent. Now we're being given a scenario where we can achieve that goal. Most of Canada, and a necessary slice of Mexico, can be in our hands within a year. Maybe Cuba will finally wise-up. We can flaunt it to China and Europe that we're still on the prowl. We're the only superpower, and we should act like it. We have to stop asking foreigners for permission to defend our national interests. Just do what we need to do!...Are you going to help?"

Deise responded by standing then stating," You know where the door is."

Poller shook his head, rose and walked towards the exit. Before stepping into the hallway he turned to Deise, "Don't blame me. Poor damn, stupid fool." Poller did not pull the door out as he departed.

After securing the locks, Deise briefly considered 'phoning the Vice President and demanding to know why Maurus set his yap dog loose; but he decided it would be a waste of time. "There's a leash between them, although it's difficult to tell who's really in control."

He went to the bedroom, picked up his briefcase and returned to the couch. Taking out a legal pad and a pen, Deise began outlining his thoughts. An hour and a half, and several drafts, later he had made his decision. "I can always go back to teaching history if the leadership doesn't appreciate my eloquence."

* * * * *

By 6AM Sean Deise had awakened from another fitful sleep. He telephoned his family at home on Staten Island. They were all early risers so there was no concern about disturbing their rest. He chatted for a few minutes, reminding his wife Kate to set the DVD recorder for WNN's local channel. Despite her request, Sean told her she would have to wait to hear his decision. "I might chicken out and go the other way at the last moment. I don't want to lock myself in. Besides the line could be tapped. There'd be no suspense if the story broke before I got to the Hill." He promised to be home for dinner.

Deise prepared himself for the morning in about twenty-five minutes. The time was shortly before 7AM; "There's a few hours . . ," he started to think when the 'phone rang. It was the Speaker on a conference call with the three other Representatives. "Good morning to everyone," said Todd Poorberry. The four responded in kind. "I've arranged for a limo to pick you up in front of the building at 7:30. Is that OK?" They all agreed. "You can come back here and barricade yourselves in your offices until the session is ready to begin. The House security staff will run interference for you with the members of the fourth estate."

The quartet met downstairs several minutes before the scheduled pick-up time. They muttered idle sports-talk while awaiting their transportation. The limo would not be able to stop directly outside the front door because of some maintenance work that was being done. The Representatives would have to walk about ten feet to the taxi stand spot. The limo came along the drive precisely at 7:30. The group proceeded out the door and across the sidewalk. Sean Deise trailed his associates. Behind him came a shout. "Hey! Look out!" Deise spun around and saw an approaching motorbike rider. He had to jump backwards to avoid being struck by the speeding biker. The person who had yelled the warning was the building's doorman, who now came running up to Deise. The rider, wearing a dark helmet and dark clothes continued his rapid pace, flying past the startled on-lookers.

"Are you alright?" inquired the doorman as he ran up to Deise.

"Yes...yes, thanks," replied the Congressman as he shook the other's hand. "I'm glad somebody was awake."

"He must be one of those messengers, although I don't remember seeing him before. They don't care who or what's in their way."

"Well, thanks again," Deise said. "If he'd hit me I'd be road pizza for sure."

"If I see him again, I'm calling the cops," the doorman assured him as the four Representatives seated themselves in the limo.

\* \* \* \* \*

## 10:51 AM

Congressman Sean Deise entered the House chamber from a side doorway. He was unaware that the three other Members had announced their support for the measure to remove Cory Stratton from the office of President. Nevertheless, he sensed a palpable tension as soon as he set foot in the chamber. A premonition stirred a belief that his was the deciding vote. He desperately wanted a drink of water, but he feared his shaking hands would not permit such a task.

Sean Deise, almost a cliché in this circumstance—the average guy who through a series of fortunate events finds himself at the epicenter of an extraordinary moment in time. Graduate of a small college near his home, returning there for a few years as an Assistant Professor of History, then married to another faculty member, now with two children, two terms in the State Assembly then drafted to run for an open House seat he wins based on his refusal to accept donations from any source outside the district. The Founders of the nation had probably envisioned that great decisions in Congress would be made by counsel of learned elders. Here now was a common man, age 45, on the verge of deciding the fate of the Republic.

Sean Deise stood before his colleagues and the nation alone in the spotlight of history. Remembering the words he had finished early in the morning, Deise reached into his coat pocket and withdrew the text. The papers fluttered as he placed them on the podium. Finally, he coughed to clear his throat. Deise began his historic judgment, "The Framers of the Constitution established Congress as the first among equals by delineating its powers and duties in Article I. 'We the People' is the opening phrase of the preamble of the Constitution. Here in the House of Representatives these two concepts come together. We are the American people's chosen representatives, elected to decide matters great and small. The President can propose lawful policy, the Supreme Court may weigh the legitimacy of policy within the context of the law, but the House along with the Senate decides what is enacted as law. The Constitution is the bedrock of the American system of law. The Amendments are refinements to that system. Because all of these transactions are undertakings of human beings, flaws creep into the proceedings. What seemed abundantly clear and straightforward at the time of passage can become vague and imprecise at some later date. What was intended for one purpose may become an instrument for an unintended alternative."

"In some democracies the selection of the head of government is determined in a swap-meet among parliamentary factions. What might be called bribery in other circumstances becomes agenda accommodation. The voters in such nations have only an indirect voice in expressing their preference for the country's top political figure. Weeks, sometimes months, are required to jury-rig what in the long run may be an illusory majority. Anyone who emerges from such a process is at the mercy of the shifting sands of capricious interests, and can be dismissed in what is called a vote of no-confidence."

"The American process has evolved far differently. We are so radical we permit the voters to elect the nation's preeminent public official. The President is chosen by the people, and can be removed by the people at a subsequent election. It was never the explicit or implicit intent of the Framers of the Constitution to subject the President's term in office to the mood swings of Congress. Most certainly Congress has the rightful duty to evaluate legislation and appointees proposed by the Chief Executive. Congress may also influence policy through measures passed or defeated. Congress cannot, must not, control the Presidency. We came dangerously close to such a catastrophe when the Radical Unionists were in the majority during the States War of the 1860s."

"The 25th Amendment was born out of the realization that a procedural gap existed in maintaining the continuity of Executive power. The Amendment was designed as a mechanism for filling a vacancy created by death or severe illness. It was never intended as a backdoor version of a no-confidence vote."

"The attempt, some would say nefarious attempt, to oust President Cory Stratton is in my mind nothing more than a cold-blooded attempt to distort the Constitution. It is nothing more, as I fear after learning the motivations of one of the plotters, than an attempted coup d'etat through misuse of the Constitution."

"I will not disgrace this House, and undermine the integrity of the Presidency, by supporting this measure. Somewhere in the debate over Mexico, Bert Maurus' personal disagreement with the President became a personal vendetta."

"I support the Constitutional principal of an independent President. I support President Cory Stratton."

"I vote No!"

# *Epilogue*

THE REACTION WITHIN the chamber of the House of Representatives was astoundingly anti-climatic. A handful of Members stood up and shouted at Sean Deise; an almost equal number arose to applaud him. The others sat in silence, either relieved or shocked that the challenge had collapsed. Speaker Poorberry made the obvious official by declaring that the measure had failed to obtain a 2/3 majority, so it was therefore defeated. The chamber began to clear slowly. The usual milling about in the aisles, the mini-news conferences in the outside hallways, the rush back to the office to sample constituent opinion—all this took place, but without the intense passion of previous days.

    The news media also seemed to draw back. When the Speaker made his announcement on the voting results, most sites jumped back to their standard presentations after a brief summary by their lead correspondent. It was if the nation had decided to shake off the residual memories of a bad dream, and go about its normal business. The fascination of so bluntly challenging a President had fed a compulsion for involvement in a unique drama, if only through the vicarious mediums of television and the web. The story had reached its climax, the central character had survived (barely), and now the routine could resume. The most severe Constitutional crossroads since the impeachment and conviction of President George Mc McClellan in March 1865 (he was charged with treason for proposing a negotiated settlement to the stalemated States War), and the subsequent domination of the Presidency by the Radical Unionists in Congress until Abraham Lincoln's inauguration in March 1869, had captivated the public's attention while it was white-hot; but with its cooling, the grubby underlying problems still remained, still required attending to, yet the public was now tired of it. Coup or not, national survival or not, the entire mix became yesterday's news in next to no time.

The remainder of Cory Stratton's term was an ordeal for the man. His narrow escape left him confronting a stark fact—a majority in the House and a plurality of the general public had endorsed the proposal to oust him from office. Stratton had to confront the bitter reality that the enthusiastic support which had made him President was gone. He was required now to begin a careful, considerate program to restore his acceptance by the people and the Congress.

※ ※ ※ ※ ※

The resignation letter of Bertford Maurus as Vice President was delivered to the Secretary of State shortly after noon on October 15th. It contained a single sentence announcing his departure. Cory Stratton did not respond publicly to Maurus' surrender of office; however, a White House spokesperson told reporters that a committee of senior Presidential advisers would begin an immediate review of suggested nominees for the vacant post of Vice President. The irony was noted: Bert Maurus' successor would be selected according to the provisions of the 25th Amendment—in this case, it would be Section 2. Within an hour of Maurus' withdrawal the eight Cabinet Secretaries who had supported him followed him once more by also submitting their resignations. On Monday,

November 1st, a week of Congressional hearings began in order to consider the President's nominee for Vice President.

The House and Senate then spent two days debating the matter, and on Thursday the 12th confirmed Donald Warsen (who had been serving as Governor of California) as the next Vice President. The President had chosen Warsen to emphasize his commitment to the Border States in the continuing Mexican crisis. Of course it helped that Warsen had been a public supporter of Stratton since the problem began.

* * * * *

Bert Maurus returned to his home near Columbus, Ohio. He said his initial plan was to rest, however he pledged to continue speaking out on national issues. Maurus denied that he planned to run for an open U.S. Senate seat the following year; he acknowledged an interest in writing a book about his experiences during the past few years. Tragically, Bert Maurus' future was cut short several months later. On the anniversary of the first border attack (which occurred on July 4, 2009 against an American security team), an unknown gunman shot and killed the former Vice President at his home. Maurus had rejected the Secret Service protection offered by President Stratton. An extensive Federal investigation failed to uncover any suspect. A FBI report stated Maurus was murdered by an assailant using a 9mm handgun. Two shots were fired after Maurus opened his door to a late evening caller.

* * * * *

Alex Poller obtained a position as a political commentator on satellite radio. (The program is "Never Call Retreat" on the Eagle network.) He repeatedly claims that Maurus was assassinated by a hit man of the Durango cartel, and that the cartel has several sleeper cells within the United States. He ends each of his broadcasts with this sign-off barrage: "We are now one day closer to Armageddon. Be alert! Watch for the signs! The dopes in Washington can't see it coming! I am doing everything I can to keep you informed about this threat!"

Poller has also announced that he has initiated the process of establishing a new national political party, to be called American Patriots Action. If the party can overcome the legal obstacles in each of the 51 States, Poller stated he hoped to be the party's Presidential candidate in 2012.

Alex Poller declined all invitations to participate in the gathering of material for this book.

\* \* \* \* \*

A multi-national force of 15,000 troops, from various Latin American countries and the United States, was deployed in and around Mexico City in the Summer of 2010. Mexico was still in considerable turmoil at the time this book was being published in December 2010.

Almost forgotten by the outside world, Canada went about its business of dissolution. The North Prairie Republic had issued a unilateral declaration of independence on October 8, 2010. The remaining Provinces and territories expressed their intent to continue in confederation—with Quebec, of course, being the exception. The Prime Minister of the NPR stated that the new nation would consider affiliating with the United States "once the political climate there cools down." As of this book's publication date no public discussions had taken place.

\* \* \* \* \*

The Congressional elections of 2010 provided Cory Stratton with a ready-made platform for political rehabilitation. Two years previously he had proposed a major overhaul of campaign finance regulations. Other concerns had pushed this topic off the stove, and not merely to the back burner. Stratton said there was an urgent need to liberate the election process from the possible corrupting influence of large donations, whether secret or not. The issue might have died of voter apathy except that the last act of the Independent Prosecutor's investigation of the De Witt Administration bore fruit in the Summer of 2010. A Federal jury convicted the Finance Chairman of Jeffrey De Witt's 1996 re-election campaign of covering up illegal contributions from an Angolan diamond consortium. It was revealed during the trail that Angola's military dictatorship had hoped to gain access to influential government officials in Washington; Angola had lost its major sponsor when the People's Republics of Eurasia imploded in the early 1990s. Angola's leaders had retained a vision of turning their nation into the dominant power in non-Arab Africa.

The trial verdict brought back to the headlines all the influence-peddling scandals which erupted during the De Witt years. Voter turnout was higher in some States than it had been at any time in the previous half century. While campaign finance reform was not the critical issue in every race, it was a dominant feature in the defeat of several candidates (incumbents and challengers in both parties) who stood firmly against revising the current system. Most notable was Senator Connor Mitchells, the Majority Leader.

\* \* \* \* \*

Where will America go from here? What will be the impact on the approaching Presidential campaign of 2012? The answers will depend on the American people. In times of crisis Americans have always responded to stand in defense of their homeland. The hard job has always been getting them to their feet in the first place. Affairs of State seem remote to the average person in this country. If all politics is local, the locals too often don't seem to care. Until the barbarians (or the usurpers, or the instigators, or the tax man) are literally at the gate, Joe and Betty America are willing to leave politics to someone who doesn't have a real life.

Yet there is hope. The 2010 election campaign seemed to awaken in voters the realization that what goes on in politics and government does matter to the real lives of ordinary people. It can no longer be a case of leave a dirty business to those willing to wallow in mud. Whether or not the public's attention will remained focused on issues of integrity and leadership will be one of the guiding factors in the fifty-seventh Presidential election of this Republic.

\* \* \* \* \*

### The actual wording of Section 4 of the 25th Amendment to the U.S. Constitution:

Whenever the Vice President and a majority of either the principal officers of the Executive department or such other body as Congress may by law provide, transmit to the President pro tempore of the Senate and the Speaker of the House of Representatives their written declaration that the President is unable to discharge the powers and duties of his office, the Vice President shall immediately assume the powers and duties of the office as Acting President.

Thereafter, when the President transmits to the President pro tempore of the Senate and the Speaker of the House of Representatives his written declaration that no inability exists, he shall resume the powers and duties of his office unless the Vice President and a majority of either the principal officers of the Executive department or such other body as Congress may by law provide, transmit within four days to the President pro tempore of the Senate and the Speaker of the House of Representatives their written declaration that the President is unable to discharge the powers and duties of his office. Thereupon Congress shall decide the issue, assembling within forty-eight hours for that purpose if not in session. If the Congress, within twenty-one days after the receipt of the latter written declaration, or, if Congress is not in session, within twenty-one days after Congress is required to assemble, determines by a two-thirds vote of both

Houses that the President is unable to discharge the powers and duties of his office, the Vice President shall continue to discharge the same as Acting President; otherwise the President shall resume the powers and duties of his office.